The Kiriov Tapes

The Kiriov Tapes

BY

OWEN SELA

PANTHEON BOOKS
A Division of Random House, New York

35798642

Copyright © 1973 by Owen Sela

All rights reserved under International and Pan-American
Copyright Conventions. Published in the United States by
Pantheon Books, a division of Random House, Inc., New York.
Originally published in Great Britain by
Hodder & Stoughton.

Library of Congress Cataloging in Publication Data

Sela, Owen.
The Kiriov Tapes.
I. Title.
[PZ4.S4618Ki3] [PR6069.E33]   823'.9'14   73–4311
ISBN 0–394–48534–3

Manufactured in the United States of America

For

JENNIFER

for more than she knows

Contents

Prologue

January 18th, 1963

"I'm sorry," the man said, "it's such short notice."

Adrian Quimper said, "That's all right."

The man said, "We've booked you on a BOAC flight this afternoon." He looked at Quimper anxiously.

Quimper asked, "Will I have diplomatic cover?"

"Only," the man said, "if it is necessary."

Quimper thought about that while he smoked a cigarette. The man pushed an ashtray across the desk.

Quimper said, "I won't be able to take a rifle, then. Perhaps I'll take a Smith and Wesson with a Pantechnic Mark 7 Sightmaster. It's good for about sixty yards."

The man said, "Whatever you like."

Quimper said, "The rifle would be more accurate. But there might be problems, taking it through customs."

The man didn't say anything.

*   *   *

The gentleman from the Embassy met him as he came out of customs. "It's good of you to come," he said, "at such short notice."

Quimper felt hot in his tweeds. He could hardly believe

9

that four hours ago he'd been in London, among snow-covered pavements and grey lighting. "It's nice here," he said, "warm."

"Yes," said the man from the Embassy. "Here in Beirut, the winters are exceptionally mild."

*   *   *

The man from the Embassy said, "It must be an interesting job. Plenty of opportunity for travel and that."

Quimper looked at him flat-eyed. "I'd rather we didn't talk," he said.

"Of course," the man from the Embassy said. "You must be nervous."

Quimper walked over to the window and checked the focus of the telescopic sight. He drew a bead on an Arab walking down the sunlit hill towards the Normandy Bar. The thin Semitic features appeared in close-up, framed in the cross hairs. Quimper lowered the gun and looked. Fifty yards, he thought. It'll do, he thought, he'd worked in much more difficult circumstances before. Beyond the hill he could see the deep blue of the Mediterranean. It was always like this. In on one plane, out on another. Never time to stop or think or see. It was a shame, Quimper thought. He liked Beirut.

*   *   *

It was twenty minutes past nine when the man from the Embassy said, "There he is."

Quimper stood behind the window and looked.

"The man in European dress. The one in the off-white two-piece suit."

He was a man of medium height, stocky, with thick dark hair. Fortyish, Quimper thought, watching the man walk slowly towards him. He walked with a kind of shuffle as if he were drunk or very tired. He had a strip of plaster on his forehead.

Deliberately Quimper stepped out on to the balcony. He had decided earlier that if he was to get it right he'd have to fire from the balcony. He took off his sunglasses and allowed his eyes to get used to the glare.

The man was seventy yards away, heading down the hill. Quimper had been told that every morning the man walked down to the Normandy Bar to collect his mail. Slowly Quimper extended the revolver and adjusted the sight.

He rested one wrist on the railing of the balcony and because he did not like mistakes, he trapped his right wrist with his left. He made sure that he was evenly balanced and looked through the sight he had checked earlier. It focused on the man's chest, picking out the buttons on his off-white suit. Quimper smiled. Everything was all right, so far.

Gradually he raised the gun so that he could see the man's face. Craggily handsome, worried, eyes heavy-lidded, slightly bloodshot. It was an intelligent face, good mouth, eyes that cared. Quimper saw the face trapped in the cross hairs of the sight and went very still. It wasn't, he thought, it couldn't be, remembering the lazy smile, the voice with the pitiful stutter. From sixty yards away through a telescopic gunsight he looked into the face of the man who had once been his friend and his finger curled on the trigger.

And froze.

PART I

"His flight was madness. When our actions do not
Our fears do make us traitors."

Shakespeare
Macbeth IV.ii.3

I

"H'M," SAID C, "INGENIOUS. VERY."

The man from the Air Ministry smiled.

"You are to be congratulated, Mr. — er — er —"

"Pnaismith," the man from the Air Ministry said, "with a silent 'p'."

"Very ingenious," C said again. He cleared his throat. "More sherry?"

Pnaismith held out his glass.

"The only problem," C said, pouring, "is who is going to do it."

The sherry ran over Pnaismith's fingers and trickled to the floor. C stopped pouring.

Pnaismith said, "I — we — rather hoped . . . you know . . ."

"Yes," said C thoughtfully, "I know. More sherry?"

Pnaismith held his glass delicately away. His fingers already felt sticky.

C stared at the decanter in his hand and said, "Now where the devil is your glass?"

"It's full sir," Pnaismith said. "Thank you."

"Drink up," C said and replaced the decanter. "Quite a problem you know. Finding the right sort of chappie."

"Yes, sir," Pnaismith said.

15

"But don't worry Mr. — er — er."

"Pnaismith."

"Don't worry. I think I know the right man."

*   *   *

"Ingenious," said David Carruthers. "Very."

"I can't hear a word you are saying. Can you speak up?"

"It's the scrambler, sir. It distorts everything."

"D. Tort did you say?" C said. "Names are getting stranger all the time. Had a fellow in called Pnaismith with a silent 'p'."

Carruthers sighed and threw the switch. "I think I know just the man, sir," he said.

"Do you Carruthers? Splendid! Well I'll leave you to get on with it then."

"I will, sir."

"Goodbye, Carruthers. I knew you'd be able to help out."

*   *   *

"I won't do it," Nicholas Maasten said. "Not on your father's life."

"As I remember," Carruthers said, "there's a small question of £5,000."

"There's also," Maasten said, "a small question of proof."

Carruthers went silent. After a while he said: "But someone's got to do it."

"I know the man," Nicholas Maasten said.

"You do?"

"He used to be with Air Charter. Harry Littledyke."

"Don't remember him," Carruthers said.

"You will," Maasten promised. "And you'll find that it all comes down to a question of money."

*   *   *

With Harry Littledyke everything came down to a question of money. There were good times when he had plenty of it, and bad times when he had none. There were also horrible in-between times when he had a little and was trying to make more.

This was one of the horrible in-between times.

"You're sure it's safe?" Harry asked.

The man with the pin-striped suit rested his hands on his briefcase and pursed his lips. After some deliberation he said, "We think so."

"I mean, I wouldn't go to jail or anything. I'm sure you mean what you say and all that, but doing a favour is one thing. I mean fourteen years is a lot to ask."

"We'll stand by you," the man with the pin-striped suit said.

Harry sipped his coffee and followed it down with a spoonful of baked jam roll. "Would you like some treacle tart?"

"No," said the man in the pin-striped suit. "Thank you."

Harry ate more of the jam roll. "The treacle tart is good," he said. "As good as you'll find at the Bristol."

"I'm sure it is," said the man in the pin-striped suit. "I simply don't happen to like treacle tart."

"Oh," said Harry. He finished the jam roll in silence and drank more coffee.

"You wouldn't, I suppose," he asked, "give me a letter or anything like that?"

"No," said the man in the pin-striped suit. "Most certainly not."

2

NOWADAYS, IT IS REALLY QUITE EASY to obtain a visa for the United States of America. All one needs are two photographs, suitable character references, some evidence of means and a valid passport, preferably that of a NATO country. British passports are particularly favoured.

All Anatol Kiriov had were the two photographs and a British passport for which he had paid £200. But that was the least of his problems.

It was six o'clock on a Saturday evening and the crew-cut young man in the dark uniform told him the visa section was shut. Visa applications could only be handled personally, the man said, when the visa section was open. It opened on Monday morning at ten o'clock.

Kiriov explained that he had been delayed by the broken fan belt on his Skoda. It wouldn't have done much good, the uniformed man said. The visa section didn't open at all, Saturdays. Of course, if there were any special urgency . . .

There was, but it wasn't anything Kiriov wanted to tell the crew-cut young man about. From where he stood, he could look down the wide sweeping steps that led to Upper Grosvenor Street. At the foot of the steps the pavement had been slenderised, forming a parking bay large enough for three Cadillac Imperials.

There were no Cadillacs parked there now. There was only a battered maroon Moskvitch and Kiriov knew that the men inside it were going to kill him.

*   *   *

Kiriov had first spotted the Moskvitch when his fan belt broke. The car had driven past him, gone on, reappeared five minutes later and parked thirty yards behind him. And there it had waited while he had walked home and collected his tools, returned to his broken-down car and repaired it. Kiriov was not good with cars. It had taken him four skinned knuckles and thirty-five minutes to replace the fan belt.

He had been on his way to the United States Embassy that Saturday afternoon because it was the only time Kiriov had been free that week. Ever since he'd decided to defect, Kiriov had been working seven days a week. As he was only indirectly involved in Intelligence, Kiriov knew that his value to the Americans was strictly marginal. So over the past few weeks he had directly set out to acquire such information as would be useful to his new friends. The fact that his information was of far more use to the British was unfortunate, but not sufficiently so to make Kiriov alter his plans. The information was of such importance that the Americans would welcome it. They would also pay far more than the British.

Originally Kiriov's visit to the American Embassy had been of a routine nature. He had wanted to find out how quickly one could get a visa to enter America, and if possible collect the necessary forms. The appearance of the Moskvitch had changed all that.

Kiriov realised that he was under suspicion. He knew also

that his colleagues had very effective methods of dealing with suspicion. Struggling with his fan belt, Kiriov had decided that his only hope lay in defecting at once. And that was the biggest difficulty.

While Kiriov had devoted a great deal of time and attention to collecting the information his friends would find invaluable, he had not, apart from having his picture taken and buying a forged passport, given thought to the sheer mechanics of defection.

Now he wished he had. After repairing his fan belt, he had managed to lose the Moskvitch in the back doubles near Camden Town. Then, more in hope than anything else, he had made straight for the American Embassy. He had not expected to find notices saying "Defectors and spies through Channel Two". But he had expected to find the Embassy open. To find someone who could deal with his problem. The uniformed crew-cut man was obviously much too young and only concerned with the security of the building.

Indeed he was now staring at Kiriov suspiciously. Ever since the student demonstrators had nearly got into the Embassy, the young man had been obsessed by nut-cases with bombs. He was thinking that Anatol Kiriov looked remarkably like a nut-case with a bomb.

"Why don't you come back Monday, bud?" he suggested tersely.

"I'll do that," Kiriov said and started to walk towards the tall glass doors underneath the golden American eagle. He didn't think the men in the waiting Moskvitch would be brazen enough to kill him on the steps of the American Embassy. At least Kiriov hoped not.

3

A MAN CLIMBED OUT of the Moskvitch. He was a squat, solid-looking fellow wearing a wide-shouldered, wide-bottomed brown suit and a flat brown hat, jammed far down over his square forehead. He opened the rear door of the Moskvitch and waved invitingly to Kiriov.

Kiriov did not wave back. His own car was parked some distance away, round the front of the Embassy. He could see no way of getting to it safely.

As Kiriov hesitated, two policemen came round the corner, part of the detail on perpetual patrol, on the pavements round the Embassy. Kiriov relaxed, and started down the steps. The man holding the door open gave him a toothless smile. Kiriov went straight towards him and at the last moment, swerved and jumped. He landed on the pavement right in front of the policemen. Both policemen looked at him with suspicious interest.

"I am sorry," Kiriov said. "Do you have the time?"

One policeman kept staring at him and sniffing. The other looked at his watch. "Twenty minutes to seven."

"Ah! Thank you. Can you tell me where is Hilton?"

"Go down to the traffic lights, turn left. It is about three hundred yards down."

Kiriov hesitated. "What traffic lights?"

"The ones behind you, sir." The policeman pointed over Kiriov's shoulder. Kiriov turned and pointed too. It was entirely coincidence that the Moskvitch came within the arc of their pointing fingers.

A door slammed. The Moskvitch scampered away from the kerb, trailing a puff of blue smoke behind its worn tyres.

Kiriov went around to the front of the Embassy where his own car was parked. He started it and drove round Grosvenor Square and down Brook Street. He was halfway down the street when the Moskvitch filled his mirror. It did more than that. It nudged him.

* * *

The Skoda shot forward. Kiriov's head shot back. The Skoda missed a taxi by a hair's breadth and rode on. Kiriov saw the traffic lights at the corner of Bond Street and wrenched the wheel to the right.

The Moskvitch followed, slabsided, predatory. As he slowed for the entrance to Piccadilly, the Moskvitch nudged him again.

This time Kiriov was prepared. He accelerated into Piccadilly and turned left. The Moskvitch charged after him, dented wing flapping. Kiriov somehow managed to get a taxi between them and stopped in the heavy traffic jamming the entrance to the Circus. The Moskvitch pulled out and drew alongside him.

"Hey! Hey!" One of the men was tapping on his window. Kiriov looked straight ahead. "Hey! Hey!" Kiriov was worried they might break the glass. The man stopped beating the glass and tried the door. Traffic began to move. Kiriov spurted into a gap. The Moskvitch followed. Crumpled nose to dented tail they went round Piccadilly Circus and down the Haymarket. Occasionally the man in the Moskvitch leaned his head out and shouted "Hey! Hey!"

Kiriov led them round Trafalgar Square twice and realised he could spend a great part of the evening being followed by a belligerent Moskvitch and a man who kept leaning out of it and shouting "Hey! Hey!" Until of course one of them ran out of petrol. Kiriov looked at his petrol gauge. It seemed that he was the one most likely to do that.

Kiriov made off up Charing Cross Road. The Moskvitch followed. Kiriov hogged two lanes to prevent them drawing alongside. Other motorists tooted in annoyance. They went round Cambridge Circus and up Tottenham Court Road. A car swerving for a parking place held up the Moskvitch and Kiriov accelerated gratefully. The Moskvitch was only a distant red reflection when he turned left into the maze of side streets behind Goodge Street underground station.

He drove past tiny Indian restaurants and crowded provision stores, passed second-hand furniture dealers with stock piled on the pavement and shabby vendors of electrical goods. He saw a pub and stopped right in front of it. There would be people in a pub. Lots of people. Even if the men in the Moskvitch found him there, they would not dare do anything.

Because he wanted to keep a clear head, Kiriov ordered a beer. Because he thought he might be there some time, he ordered one pint. He stood at the counter and sipped the heavy, dark brown liquid. If the Americans were closed till Monday he decided, he had no option but to defect to the British. The only problem was how.

He hadn't arrived at a solution when the two men from the Moskvitch came in. They were of the same height and identically dressed. From under the flat brown hats they gave him identical toothless grins.

Kiriov looked hurriedly away. There was a distinguished-looking gentleman beside him, with a monocle and a green suede waistcoat.

"How goes the cricket?" Kiriov asked. "Did Australia score many wickets?"

A spiky grey eyebrow curled incredulously over a steel-rimmed monocle. "*Ich spreche nicht Englisch,*" the man said. "*Sprechen Sie Deutsch?*"

Kiriov smiled glassily. "How is your Chancellor?" he asked.

The German shook his head. "*Nein. Nein. Sprechen Sie Deutsch?*"

Kiriov scratched his head and said, "*Nein.*"

The men from the Moskvitch moved across the opposite side of the bar to him. They weren't grinning now.

Kiriov tapped his glass and smiled disconsolately at the German. "*Ist gute?*"

"*Nein, nein,*" the German said and tapped his brandy and ginger ale.

The barman with commendable alacrity topped them both up.

A cheery, milling crowd thrust its way through the doors. They were celebrating an out-of-season football match, waving flags and wearing rosettes and long coloured scarves that trailed and got in everyone's way. They jostled happily round the bar clapping each other on the back with shouts of "Where's Bert?", "Did Harry get here?" and "Where's the little bugger got to?"

The German drank his brandy, clicked his heels and said, "*Danke schön. Guten abend.*"

Kiriov clicked his heels and spilled some of his beer.

24

4

THE CHEERY BEER-SWILLING CROWD formed an impenetrable barrier between Kiriov and the men from the Moskvitch. Kiriov had another beer and wondered how he could get out of the pub and how he could defect to the British. Two beers later, Kiriov had quite another problem.

Three pints of rapidly drunk bitter was just as rapidly filling his bladder and Kiriov did not dare visit the gents. He had no doubt that the two men from the Moskvitch would follow him there, and in the privacy of that pungent, dimly lit place there was no knowing what they would do to him.

Kiriov shifted about uneasily and stared. Because he could not remain there staring at an empty glass, he drank vodka. The first drink eased his discomfort and Kiriov concluded that vodka had some special chemical effect on beer. It had. He began to sweat profusely and soon there was a gentle haze over the crowd and the bar and the two men from the Moskvitch opposite.

More people came in. The air became quite thick with shouting and with cigarette smoke. Someone bought drinks for everyone else and a brimming tankard of lager was thrust into Kiriov's face. He sipped at it and drank more vodka and his bladder began to hurt. He could feel it swelling inside

25

him, distended like a football, growing larger every second. He knew that if he didn't do something about it damn quick it would burst.

Kiriov sprinted for the door. His two companions saw him move and came after him. But there were two of them and they had to come the long way round. By the time they had upset a couple of beers, apologised and tripped over a scarf, Kiriov was gone.

But not far. Doubled up with his effort Kiriov had got the Skoda moving unsteadily down the narrow street. The two men ran clumsily to the Moskvitch and went after him.

Kiriov saw the Moskvitch take off like a lumbering bat and groaned. Somehow he had hoped for a bigger start than that.

Then he saw something that would reduce his lead even more. The crossroads ahead of him were blocked by four cars, waiting patiently for the lights to change.

Kiriov lifted off. The single undamaged headlamp of the Moskvitch ballooned in his mirror. The traffic lights went from red to amber. Kiriov accelerated. Amber to green. The cars ahead of him moved, sweeping left into the four-lane one-way system. Kiriov checked his mirror. The Moskvitch was catching him fast.

He sped up to the crossing, the Moskvitch closing right up as he braked for the compulsory left turn. Helpfully he flicked his trafficator to the left. Then Kiriov turned savagely right.

A Mini travelling fast towards Kiriov, flared its headlamps and swerved. Kiriov swung beside it, avoided an oncoming Merc and tried for the inside lane. He was going the wrong direction down a one-way drag strip. Cars were zooming at him with blaring horns and flaming headlights. Kiriov dodged and turned, coping frantically. He bounced on the pavement for a few yards, scattering pedestrians. There were shouts and people thumped angrily on the roof of the Skoda. Then Kiriov bumped back on to the road bringing a double-decker to a grinding stop. A BMW passing the double-decker hurled itself sideways to avoid him. A Jaguar came to a tyre-shedding stop. Kiriov charged between them, frightened, feeling surrounded by the wall of screaming metal and blaring lights, hoping he could get out of this frightening madness. He saw a little blue light by the side of the road and headed directly for it. As usual, the most obvious solution was the best.

He grabbed the extreme right lane and accelerated down it, turning on his own lights. Just outside the police station he spied a gap between two patrol cars and made for that.

The Skoda slammed solidly into the pale blue 1100, shifting it six feet back. Glass shattered, metal clanged and twisted. Kiriov hit the roof of the Skoda and watched its bonnet curl. He bumped his head on the windscreen, and then the car lights went out and all movement ceased. All Kiriov could feel was the pain and the pressure inside him.

He clambered urgently out of the Skoda and rushed up the steps into the police station. There was a pleasant-looking constable at the desk.

"Sir," Kiriov gasped, "please! I have to do a piss."

Sergeant Albert Lawrence moved beside the constable. Sergeant Lawrence had been in the police force for twenty-two years. During his years of service, Sergeant Lawrence had dealt with card sharps, prostitutes, car thieves, pimps, bustle punchers, breakers and con men. He could recognise a drunk when he saw one, especially one who was about to pee on his polished station floor. He gestured to the constable to take Kiriov downstairs.

5

KIRIOV CAME BACK SMILING and feeling rather ashamed of himself. Also the station floor wouldn't keep still. He came up to Sergeant Lawrence, happily.

"You are Chief Officer?"

"Yes," Sergeant Lawrence said.

Kiriov smiled. "Good. We have drink. Yes?"

"You have had too much already," Sergeant Lawrence said darkly. "Is that your vehicle out there?"

Kiriov half turned to look down the steps and decided the effort was too much. He wouldn't be needing a car any more. "Yes. It is for you. You keep it."

Sergeant Lawrence asked, "Have you just come down Tottenham Court Road from the north?"

"North, south, what difference! We are friends! Brothers!" Kiriov held out his hand. "East, west, make no difference, underneath all same. *Ja!*" Kiriov stared at his outstretched palm as if he was seeing it for the first time. "No difference," he muttered and let the arm drop limply back.

Sergeant Lawrence told the constable, "You had better take him into the charge room." The constable took Kiriov by the arm and started to lead him away. Kiriov went without protest. He desperately needed to sit down and it was only when he saw that Sergeant Lawrence was not coming with them that he turned and shouted, "You come quick. *Ja.* We talk. *Ja.*"

Kiriov felt quite content in the charge room. It was warm and he could sit. He could also relax and give in to that pleasant euphoria that befogged his brain. He wondered if he should sing. He started humming a tune and realised he only knew the first four bars. He looked at the constable. The constable didn't seem to mind. Kiriov went back to the beginning and started the first of the four bars. Perhaps if he repeated it often enough, he would remember the fifth one.

It was some while before Sergeant Lawrence came into the charge room. He had checked the damage to the two cars, found out which doctor was on call and entered details of the incident in the station log book.

Kiriov caught sight of Lawrence and smiled beatifically. He liked Lawrence. After all Lawrence was his first link with the people to whom he would ultimately defect. "Hullo," Kiriov said. "Now, we talk."

Sergeant Lawrence was carrying a little bag. He held out a mouthpiece to Kiriov. "First," Sergeant Lawrence said, "we blow."

Kiriov was obliging. He grabbed the mouthpiece and blew hard into it. The crystals of the breathalyser turned a vivid blue. "Take away balloon," Kiriov said. "Now sit down. Now we talk."

To Kiriov's relief the nice fat policeman went behind the desk and sat down. Then *he* talked. "I would like you to take a blood test," Sergeant Lawrence said, "and a urine test. If you agree the police doctor will take the samples. You may if you wish have your own doctor present. If you refuse the test you could be fined and disqualified from driving."

29

Sergeant Lawrence extended his hand across the desk. "Your driving licence please."

Kiriov felt his happiness disappear. He struggled to his feet. The police constable grabbed him and pushed him back into his chair.

"No," Kiriov cried, "No. You do not understand. You do not understand."

In a firm voice Sergeant Lawrence repeated, "Your licence please."

Kiriov said, "I have no licence. I am a diplomat." He fumbled with an inside jacket pocket and pulled out a passport. "Now please, we talk."

Sergeant Lawrence gave him a tired smile. "First the licence," he said quietly, "then the blood test. *Then* we'll talk."

"You bloody stupid fool!" Kiriov cried. "I don't want a blood test. I want asylum."

Sergeant Lawrence reached and took the passport from Kiriov's trembling fingers. After twenty-two years in the force he had a large and nasty problem. He did not know how large or how nasty until two hours later.

6

Two HOURS LATER, Sergeant Lawrence felt he would never get rid of Anatol Kiriov.

The instant Kiriov had proved he had diplomatic status, Sergeant Lawrence had informed the station officer. The station officer had advised Sergeant Lawrence to have the necessary tests taken and to prepare a report for submission to the Embassy the next morning. The station officer was irritated. After all, he pointed out, this was perfectly normal procedure. But, Sergeant Lawrence protested, the man wanted asylum and there was no normal procedure for that. That, he was told, wasn't his problem. He should get in touch with the Special Branch.

The Special Branch said it wasn't their problem either. What Sergeant Lawrence should do was talk to the Home Office. Very gently, because once he started shouting he would keep on shouting, because he should have been off duty an hour ago, because it was hot and steamy inside the charge room and he was developing an itch, Sergeant Lawrence very gently mentioned that it was past midnight and the Home Office was shut. The Special Branch advised him to try anyway. There was usually someone around for emergencies.

31

If there was someone around for emergencies, he had found something better to do at half past twelve on a Saturday night. Only the concierge was there and he asked whether it couldn't wait till Monday morning. It couldn't, Sergeant Lawrence said. He was here in a hot and steamy charge room with a drunken diplomat who kept humming the same four-bar tune over and over again and if he did it once more Sergeant Lawrence would go mad or something. The Home Office said there was nothing they could do about that, but if it was a question of asylum, why didn't Sergeant Lawrence call Broadmoor.

It was at that moment the two elegantly dressed men walked into the charge room, looking as if they owned the police station and said that they had come to collect the prisoner.

Kiriov stood up to go and had to be restrained by the constable.

Because he was tired and because he was irritated and because he would much rather have been in The Feathers across the road, Sergeant Lawrence would have bawled out his favourite brother. These two men were something special. He disliked the cut of their clothes, the compact way they walked, the superior air with which they looked round the charge room. He disliked the way they spoke to him as if he were a woolly on traffic duty, and most of all he disliked the fact that both men wore guns. Sergeant Lawrence felt certain that neither of them had a licence to do so.

"All right," Sergeant Lawrence said, "let's see your warrant cards."

It was the taller one who spoke. The one with the long blond hair and who called himself Amory. "We didn't say we were from the Special Branch. We said Special Branch sent us."

32

"For what?" Sergeant Lawrence's tone implied that he could think of a dozen things, none of them complimentary.

Amory's smile was patronising. "You've done a fine job," he said, "we'll take over now."

"Like bloody hell you will," Sergeant Lawrence said. For better or worse the Russian was his prisoner. He had missed his dinner and he had missed P.C. Tibb's farewell party. He'd been on duty an hour and a half too long but he was damned if he was going to let a prisoner go with either of these two jumped-up pansies.

Amory spoke again. "Look," he said, "Let me explain. You called Special Branch, right? Well they sent us to collect your prisoner."

"You have a letter or something?"

"My dear fellow," Amory said, "in our kind of work we don't write letters. Or leave visiting cards." His tone somehow implied that his kind of work was far more serious and far more arduous than Sergeant Lawrence's.

"Unless you can provide proper authority," Sergeant Lawrence said, "he stays here."

Kiriov began to hum. They waited hoping he had found a fifth bar. He stopped and smiled shyly at Amory.

"But we've got to question him," Amory said.

Sergeant Lawrence flung out a pudgy hand in a gesture of invitation. "Go ahead."

"Alone," Amory said.

"Not on your bloody nelly."

Half an hour later the position was still unresolved. Sergeant Lawrence had got quite red in the face and had sent out for one mug of hot sweet tea. Amory smoked two Dunhills delicately selected from a sterling silver case. His companion

33

hoisted a haunch on to a radiator and began to clean his nails. Kiriov continued to hum.

It was then that Amory decided to call Adrian Quimper.

And as far as Sergeant Lawrence was concerned, that was the last straw.

7

ADRIAN QUIMPER SAT by his brother's skeleton, picked up the telephone and heard Amory say, "Adrian, is that you?"

"Yes."

"I'm sorry to disturb you. Can you get to a scrambler?"

"Don't be ridiculous," Adrian snapped. "I'm at my brother's. Even *I* don't have a scrambler."

"I need your help," Amory said. "I am at Tottenham Court Road police station."

"They're all nice chaps," Quimper said. "I'll come round and bail you out in the morning."

"For goodness' sake, Adrian, this isn't a joke! Can you get round here right away?"

"Why?"

"There's an Ivan I want sprung. It's top priority."

Adrian sighed. From below him came the gentle rumble of conversation and the faint strains of a Bach concerto. Here in his brother Hugh's study, surrounded by leather-bound medical books and numerous framed diplomas, he felt somehow peaceful.

"Adrian, will you come? It is urgent!"

"If it's that, I'll come."

"Be seeing you, then," Amory said and put the phone down.

Adrian slumped in the chair and made a face at the skeleton. He didn't really want to leave Hugh's dinner party. There were chaps there whom he hadn't seen in years, chaps who had been with him and Hugh at the school their father had run in Devon.

It was interesting how they had all ended up. Bob Latimer in advertising, Chubby Prendergast, who had flown Lancasters over Germany and got a D.S.O., now headed a toy manufacturing company. Shriver, the so stylish opening batsman, was now a director of a merchant bank and Desmond Stead still wore a sports jacket and flannels, and still left his red hair uncombed and lectured in economics.

There was also Hugh. Hugh had always been brilliant. Hugh could always have done anything he wanted to do. Hugh had chosen to be a surgeon.

They had all in their various ways done well. Comfortably off, married, speaking of children and schools and au pairs, of holidays in Brittany and the crippling effect of strikes. Quimper thought he too could have been like that.

He got up and patted the skeleton on the skull. The past was past and he couldn't change it. He went downstairs and stood hesitantly in the doorway. Hugh excused himself from a colleague from St. Godric's hospital and came over. "Anything wrong?"

"No," Adrian said, "but I have to leave now," hating the concern that flooded into his brother's eyes. Hugh always worried about him, Hugh had always felt responsible, especially since Beirut.

"Will you be all right?" Hugh asked.

Adrian wished that there was some way of telling Hugh that everything was all right, that he could never be in

36

danger again. "Everything will be fine," he said. "Say good-bye to the others for me. I will come round next week and have a look at the rockery."

"Do that," Hugh said. "Come to tea and perhaps we'll go and see a film afterwards. Noelene and I haven't been out for ages."

"You can say that again," Noelene said, walking busily up with them, smiling, her face still pert, her figure still slim despite her forty-five years and bearing three children. "Bring Carey with you, Adrian," she said.

"Perhaps," Adrian said.

"Or whoever the current girlfriend is."

"Girls come a little difficult at my age."

"Nonsense, Adrian, I'm sure you have dozens hidden away in your flat in Bayswater."

"When I get home tonight," Adrian promised, "I'll look."

Noelene laughed and stretched up and kissed him on the cheek. "Take care, Adrian," she said. Ever since Hugh had told her what Adrian Quimper had done for a living, she too had learnt the habit of concern.

8

EVEN THOUGH THEY HAD TRIED to hush it up, Sergeant Lawrence knew all about Adrian Quimper. Sergeant Lawrence had no doubt that Adrian Quimper was a disgrace to the police force. Sergeant Lawrence knew that inevitably there were policemen who were lazy and policemen who were careless. There were policemen who were inefficient and even sometimes policemen who were stupid. With an uncharacteristic generosity Sergeant Lawrence was prepared to accept them all. The only kind of policemen he could not stand were the bent ones. And he had no doubt that Adrian Quimper had been bent.

For quite some time he had been on earners from Luigi Scallo, and Quimper could count himself extraordinarily lucky not to go inside when Luigi Scallo had been sent down for seven years. It may be that they had wished to protect the good name of the service or that they did not have sufficient proof. But Sergeant Lawrence had all the proof he needed. Why else, two days after giving evidence at Scallo's trial, had Detective Inspector Adrian Quimper resigned?

Sergeant Lawrence recognised Quimper the moment he came into the charge room. He had grown older, the brown hair around the temples had turned quite grey. Quimper looked thicker set and he had, since leaving the police, grown a thick moustache. Sergeant Lawrence thought the moustache made Quimper look very different, which was just as well. His former colleagues would not want to recognise him.

He watched Quimper come into the charge room accompanied by the blond man who wasn't from the Special Branch. Quimper's presence in his charge room made Sergeant Lawrence very angry, and he determined that whatever they wanted he would stop them, just to show that they should not associate with a villain like Quimper.

*   *   *

Quimper sensed the hostility the moment he walked into the charge room. It was there as intangible as mist, hovering over the sparse furniture, imprinted upon the hard faces of the men in the room.

Amory said, "This is Sergeant Lawrence. Adrian Quimper." He nodded to a man leaning against the radiator by the window : "Harvey Milner."

Milner did not move. "Pleased to meet you," Milner said looking quickly at Quimper.

Quimper stiffened, feeling a tension that had nothing to do with the hostility in the room. There was something dangerous about Milner, something that reminded Quimper of a spring wound tight enough to snap. He remembered that he hadn't vetted Milner and that normally he vetted everyone, including R Section operatives.

"New are you?" Quimper asked.

"That's a mighty interesting way of putting it."

Quimper placed the accent. American definitely but overlayed with the lilt of France, the clipped terseness of Germany. "We must meet soon," Quimper said.

Harvey Milner just smiled.

Quimper turned to Lawrence. "I hope you can help us," he said.

Lawrence glared at him stubbornly. "I will do what I can."

"We would like to talk to this gentleman alone." Quimper nodded his head at Kiriov. "We would like to take him away with us where we can talk to him privately."

"You know I can't do that, Mr. Quimper. I can't let him go until he's stone-cold sober. If he was the ordinary sort of chummy I'd have booked him by now. Because he's a diplomat I'll just have to keep him until he's sober and then deliver him to his Embassy. Tomorrow I will let them have a report."

"We'd rather you didn't," Quimper said.

Sergeant Lawrence smiled : "You know the rules as well as I do, Mr. Quimper. Surely you wouldn't want me to bend them ?"

Quimper caught the emphasis on the word bend and stifled a quick spasm of temper. "It is important that we have an opportunity of talking to this man."

"You can talk to him here. Beyond that there is nothing I can do to help."

Quimper asked : "Tell me, did you record this incident in the log book ?"

Sergeant Lawrence nodded.

"There isn't any chance, I suppose, of deleting the entry ?"

"Not a chance in the world."

"I see," Quimper said and picked up the telephone.

Sergeant Lawrence moved to grab the phone and stopped. "Whom are you calling ?"

Quimper took out a black notebook and looked at a list of numbers on the inside cover. He dialled and asked for Chief Superintendent Templeton.

Chief Superintendent Templeton did not relish being

40

woken at one thirty in the morning. Neither did he relish
being asked if he could go to a scrambler phone.

"Damn it man, I'm only a policeman. Not bloody James
Bond."

Quimper laughed. "A favour, Jack."

Templeton listened while Quimper told him succinctly
what he wanted. Then he said: "Are you sure?"

"We can't be sure until we've spoken to him. But it could
be big, Jack. It could be really important."

"But there are rules."

"The prisoner won't mind if they're broken."

Jack Templeton was a good administrator. He was used to
making decisions and doing so quickly. Besides he'd liked
Adrian Quimper and thought it was a damn shame about the
Scallo affair. Finally he said: "All right. You can take the
man and I'll hold up the report to the Embassy until you can
get me the proper authority. But I won't do anything about
the log book."

"Thanks, Jack," Quimper said.

"Let me speak to Lawrence."

Quimper handed the phone to the policeman.

Lawrence listened, his face growing tight. If Adrian Quimper was on such intimate terms with a man like Jack
Templeton, Sergeant Lawrence felt there could be no justice
left in the world. He slammed the phone down and said:
"All right. Take him."

Amory took the Russian's arm and Quimper turned to
follow. That was why Quimper didn't know exactly what
happened next. He thought he heard Harvey Milner mutter
something that might have been: "So long copper."

Then Sergeant Lawrence barked: "You!"

Milner paused in front of the desk, going very still. Only
his eyes moved, searching Lawrence's face. Quimper recognised

the stance, feet slightly spread apart, weight evenly balanced on both feet, legs slightly bowed at the knees, arms clear of the body, jacket swinging open. Quimper noticed how naturally Milner had adopted that position and wanted to shout a warning. But it was too late.

Sergeant Lawrence had already asked "Do you have a licence for that gun?"

What happened next was too quick for the eye to follow. One moment Milner was standing there, lithely balanced in front of Lawrence's desk. The next there was a smooth blur of movement and he had a Colt .45 automatic out and was pointing it hardly three inches from Lawrence's face.

"Look in there, copper," Milner said softly. "There's my licence."

It was a joke in deplorable taste. Only Quimper noticed that the hammer on the gun was drawn back and there was only the tremor of a thumb stopping Sergeant Lawrence's brains being blown all over West Central 2.

"Harvey," Amory said, "cool it."

Milner kept staring at Lawrence. After a while he smiled and took two steps back. Despite his arrogance, Quimper had to admire the way Milner moved, cat-footed, his free arm reaching behind him for clearance and balance, his eyes never leaving Lawrence. When he was out of grabbing distance he holstered the gun in a quick smooth movement.

Quimper waited until they had left the room and looked across at Lawrence.

"I'm sorry," he said. "He's new."

Sergeant Lawrence said, "Go to hell. All of you!"

*   *   *

By the time Quimper came out of the police station, the others were crowding around a yellow Porsche. Amory was

42

helping the diplomat to climb over the tipped up front seat and Milner was already seated behind the wheel.

"Adrian," Amory said, "one more favour. Could you drive the Skoda back to our garage?"

"And how do I get home?"

"Take a taxi back. Charge it to expenses."

And that would take an extra half an hour. Quimper hesitated. He was really anxious to get home. It had been a long evening and he felt a desperate need to be alone. He wanted nothing more than to get back to his flat and listen to some music, Brahms perhaps, and then to sleep. But his sense of obligation was stronger. He sighed and said "All right," and then he remembered there was something else he had to do.

He walked round the Porsche to the driver's door. "What the hell do you think you were doing back there?" he demanded.

Milner turned slowly to look at him. "That bastard was asking for it. He was needling us right through. If he'd have been with me in Vietnam I'd have fragged him."

"In England," Quimper said tersely, "we don't use guns. Or grenades. And we have our own way of stopping people who do."

Milner smiled tightly up at him. "They'd better be good," he said in a low voice. "They'd better be pretty damn good," and with a shrilly scream of tyres catapulted the Porsche away from the kerb.

9

MILNER SLOWLY ACCELERATED up Tottenham Court Road
and turned right, picking up the reverse one-way system that
would take them back to Bedford Square and the Department.

"What's with that guy, Quimper?" Milner asked. "Whose
side is he on?"

"Ours," Amory said firmly. "Quimper's OK. He used to
be in R Section."

Milner asked "What's he do now?"

"Security, police liaison, that kind of thing."

Milner asked, "Doesn't he know he's past it? That he's got
kind of soft?"

Amory said, "It happens to all of us, Harvey. It could even
happen to you."

"I can't stand bastards who don't know where they're at.
They make it dangerous for you and me. Get what I mean?"

Amory spoke softly. "I'm not sure that I do."

"Did a job once with someone like Quimper. Too old and
too soft and drank too much to cover it up. His goddamn
hand shook so much he couldn't hit the Yankee Stadium with
a shotgun."

"Adrian isn't like that," Amory said and added pointedly,
"I like Quimper." Harvey Milner took the point.

Amory asked Milner to park in Bedford Square. There was no need for their passenger to know exactly where the Department was situated. Then he asked Milner to bring his car round, to arrange a relief for eight thirty the following morning and to check if the flat was free. The flat was a safe house the Department used for private meetings and for keeping people like their passenger on ice. Occasionally a member of R Section had other uses for it, and that reminded Amory that he hadn't phoned Sue. He lit a cigarette and thought it was a damn shame, but she would have to wait till morning.

The Russian behind him began to hum a monotonous tune that had only four bars to it. Amory let him hum. After all they were going to have the rest of the night to talk.

*   *   *

The flat was in Kilburn, in one of those turn-of-the-century developments built before anyone thought the Irish and the West Indians would treat the mother country as being more than a bit of imperial rhetoric. They got to the flat in a turn-of-the-century lift, decorated like a boudoir, with buttoned, cushioned walls and a gilt grill. It moved with slow and erratic majesty. Inside the flat, the primitive central heating burbled.

Amory let Kiriov precede him into the flat. It was a small, gloomy place, with furniture that was too big for the rooms.

Kiriov stopped in the living room and smiled at Amory. The alcoholic phase was over and he had had snatches of sleep in the police station and afterwards in the car. There was only a slight staleness in his mouth and everything had gone better than he had so hurriedly planned.

The man Amory undoubtedly worked for British Intelligence. He was nice, too. Kiriov had liked the way he had

45

stood up for his friend. It was a hopeful beginning. Kiriov said, "I am glad we are together." He meant that.

Amory took out his gun, a Walther PPK. "Get your clothes off," he said.

"I am sorry. I do not —"

"Your clothes. Take them off."

Kiriov came wide awake. "But excuse me —"

Amory gestured impatiently with the gun. Kiriov thought Amory might not be such a nice man after all and undressed.

Amory gave him a bath robe and took all his clothes. Still covering Kiriov with the gun he emptied the pockets, checked the lining, checked the labels on the clothes (they were Russian), and noticed that Kiriov had no weapons of any kind.

"All right," he said. "Now that I know who you are, my name is Amory." He put away the gun and sat down. "You can get dressed if you like," he said. "But if you are comfortable in the bathrobe, stay in it. We're going to be here for some time."

Kiriov crossed his bare legs and said he would remain in the bathrobe. Amory fixed them both vodka and tonics and said, "All right Mr. Kiriov. Let's get started. You want asylum. Why?"

"Yes, I want asylum," Kiriov said.

Amory repeated, "Why?"

Kiriov asked, "Can you give me asylum? I mean, you have the authorisation?"

Amory said, "No. I cannot guarantee anything."

"Then I talk to someone else, yes!"

"You talk to me first," Amory said. Kiriov was going to be R Section's catch. "If we like each other, then I will make a recommendation. Why do you want asylum?"

Kiriov sat back in the chair and sipped his drink. He had

46

planned for questions such as this. "I want more," he said. "I want guaranteed exit to a neutral country. And protection. Also, I want money."

"How much money?" Amory asked. The Department had to compete with every other government organisation for funds. They never had enough money.

"Thirty thousand pounds."

Amory said, "We can always send you back to the Russians."

Kiriov was unperturbed. He knew what he had to sell and how much it was worth. "That would be a pity," he said. "For me and for you. If you send me back, they will kill me. And you will also lose something."

"What?" Amory asked.

"For that," Kiriov said, "you must agree to the conditions." He smiled hesitantly. "Yes?"

That was as far as Amory got that first night. Kiriov refused to say more and refused to alter his conditions one jot. If he was in Kiriov's position, Amory thought, he would have been frightened, he would have been begging for protection on any terms. But Kiriov wasn't like that at all. He was just too damned sure.

IO

AMORY MET ANGUS MCGREGOR at nine fifteen the next morning in an establishment along Kilburn High Road, known as Mick's Cafe. Mick's Cafe smelt of chicory coffee, bacon and hot fat. At Mick's Cafe you could have two eggs and chips, eggs, bacon and chips, eggs, bacon and baked beans and chips or simply bacon and chips.

"You will not be wanting chips?" Mick asked incredulously. "Both of you?"

"No," McGregor said from behind Amory. "No chips."

"A slice of bread and butter then?"

"And two teas," Amory said.

"You siddown," Mick said. "I'll bring them to you." At quarter past nine in the morning Mick's Cafe experienced a lull. The morning breakfasts were mostly eaten and the currant bun and tea rush did not start till nearly eleven o'clock. If you ate at Mick's Cafe at around nine o'clock in the morning he would bring the food to you himself. If he liked you.

Now he flicked an Embassy into his mouth and put his head through the serving hatch. "Two eggs and bacon," he said in a voice that blasted through the cafe, "and no chips!"

He lit the cigarette and glowered at Amory and McGregor.

McGregor and Amory sat at a square formica-topped table and moved the sugar and encrusted sauce bottles to one side. "He's confident," Amory said. "He is very confident."

"He must be," McGregor replied. "Asylum and thirty thousand pounds." McGregor was the deputy head of the Department. He was a big, heavily built man with a shock of red hair and a hard, square flat face that had something Chinese about the eyes. In the Department they called him the Mandarin. Above McGregor there was only C. Amory had never met C.

"I think he is levelling with us," Amory said. "He's shrewd. He knows the value of what he has got."

"Did you threaten to send him back?" McGregor asked.

Amory nodded. "At first he said it would be a bad thing for both of us. This morning he changed his tune. He wants to go over to the Americans."

"Does he now?"

"Yes," Amory said. "He thinks the Americans will pay him more."

"He has got an infernal cheek," McGregor said and stared hard at Amory. "I suppose we had better talk to the Home Office about the drunken driving. Anyone hurt?"

"Damage to a police car," Amory said. "That's all."

"If he wants to go to the Americans," McGregor demanded, "why couldn't he smash up one of their cars?" McGregor shook his head, "It isn't going to be easy."

"No," Amory said.

"Did he have anything on him, documents, anything like that?"

"No, sir, he's clean. It's all in his head."

McGregor said, "I suppose I'll have to talk to C about asylum."

"And the money. He wants that."

49

"He has got an infernal cheek," McGregor repeated and leant back to enable Mick to lay steaming plates of bacon and eggs before them. Mick took his thumb out of the bread and slipped a plate between them, slopped down mugs of tea.

Amory began to eat hungrily.

"Good God!" McGregor exclaimed. "What's that?"

"It's bacon."

"It's not bacon, Amory, it's fat. Bacon has thin reddish strips in it. This is fat." Delicately McGregor speared one of the eggs. "I know bacon when I see it, Amory," he said.

"I like fat," Amory said, eating.

McGregor ate rapidly without relish. "How is Mr. Kiriov taking the strain?" he asked.

"As well as can be expected."

"Who's with him now?"

"Heathcote. He will be relieved at two and I will go back at six thirty."

"Fine," McGregor said. "I will get a couple of our chaps to talk to him." He stood up at the same time pressing Amory back into his seat. "We will keep in touch," McGregor said. He made a wry face. "Finish your breakfast."

As soon as McGregor had gone Amory ate his breakfast and called Sue.

"At this time of the morning," she cried, "but darling! I'm working!"

"You can always work tomorrow," Amory said. He could visualise her frown, the pencil patting the white teeth between the parted lips.

"I don't know," she said hesitantly.

"Go on," Amory said. "Girls are always getting ill and staying away from work."

"How would you know, darling?" she asked. Her laugh

caught at him. Susan, he thought, was twisting him inside out.

"Experience," he said. "And I don't want to enlarge it."

"You had better not," Susan warned and agreed to meet him at her flat in an hour.

* * *

Amory was already in bed when Sue came, curtains drawn against the watery sunlight, the cassette recorder on the bedside table hissing out Bacharach. Sue was wearing an open-necked shirt and a mini-skirt that showed off her long, slim body and the long, delicious legs. He felt his breath catch as she came over to the bed and kissed him.

"Darling, what happened last night?"

He pulled her to him, pleased at her concern, brushing her lips with his. She buried her head against his chest and Amory, hugging her to him, nuzzled his cheek against the mass of brown hair. She wasn't wearing a bra underneath her shirt and he could feel her breasts, soft and lively, pressing against him.

"I was working," he said. "Something happened unexpectedly."

Sue knew that he couldn't talk about his work. "Is it over now?" she asked, drawing away from him, fingers rapidly unbuttoning her shirt.

"No," Amory said, trying not to see the disappointment in her eyes, "not yet." He reached out and eased the shirt off her shoulders, watching her breasts writhe free. Wordlessly he pulled her across him, feeling the coolness of her body against his nakedness. His fingertips caressed the soft smoothness of her back. "We've got all day," he murmured. "All day."

II

MARKOVIC WAS SUFFERING from a hangover. His head throbbed, his throat felt as if it had been rubbed over with sandpaper, and there was a strange hot wet feeling about his eyes, as if they were melting. Markovic was a sad-faced man with a lugubrious drooping moustache and sparse brown hair. As he sat staring at the garden bounded by the high wall, he looked sadder than ever. He was thinking that he didn't want to be involved. Especially if he had to drink so much.

He didn't know why he had been singled out to meet with the Englishman. He knew nothing about aircraft. He was an analyst and here in England, he had enough figures to analyse. The English were naïve. The amount of information they published was beyond belief. Markovic thought there was something nice about that, not to be secretive all the time.

Markovic sighed and grimaced because it hurt his throat. He liked the English. They were a refined people, with a marvellous, undefinable quality, which if Markovic only knew the word he would have described as decency. Also, Markovic liked the English climate. The winters, unlike those at home, were mild, and the summers temperate. He liked the mist and the dampness and the perpetual soft rain. He liked being able to listen to the kind of music they played all day on Radio 1 and he liked the freedom to buy things without the necessity of putting his name down on a list and waiting for half a year.

Markovic did not relish the thought of being expelled from England. He did not want to return to the drabness of life and the drabness of work at the Ministry of Agriculture. It was perhaps because he had been no more than a clerk in the Ministry of Agriculture and because, knowing everything, they suspected that he had the occasional revisionist thought, they had picked him. They had also picked him because they had decided he was expendable.

Markovic wished that even if they thought that, he didn't have to drink so much.

Last night he had been with the Englishman and he had got very drunk. He belched acidly at the thought. And worse than that, last night Markovic had danced. He had danced in public. On a table. And even that had not been the end of his shamelessness.

As he had been instructed to, Markovic met the Englishman at his club. It was not one of those splendid places where they did odd things to you with black balls before they let you join. Le Chic Chick was a completely different type of club. There was music with a heavy pronounced beat, and there was lighting that was as dim and red as that of a cinema when the film is just about to start. There were chairs and tables in disorderly array, a bar, and a stage. Best of all there were girls.

A girl had been dancing on the low stage at one end of the room, coloured spotlights flickering over her, green and blue and bronze. She had been naked except for a G-string of linked metal. Espionage, Markovic had decided, was not without its compensations.

The Englishman's rapt stare signified he was four drinks

53

ahead. He was a chubby, sweaty little man with large teeth. Five o'clock shadow darkened his chin and his eyes were large, looking as if they were being pressed out by the fat on his face. He was far less dramatic than Markovic had expected.

"Good evening, Mr. Littledick," Markovic said.

"Dyke," said the Englishman with the irritable air of one who had made the explanation countless times before. "The name's Littledyke. Little as in poco, Dyke what Dutch boys are always getting their fingers into."

Markovic frowned and sat down. He hadn't quite understood the allusion to little boys. Perhaps the Englishman was trying to compromise him. He'd heard they often did that and they took photographs and threatened you with blackmail afterwards.

"I am Markovic," he said cautiously and added, "second assistant secretary."

"I suppose you'd better have a drink," Littledyke said.

Markovic watched the champagne bubbles rise, glow red and burst.

Littledyke added something black and treacly. "Cheers," he said. "To us."

Markovic drank, Russian style, tossing the liquid to the back of his throat.

"Christ!" Littledyke said.

Markovic put the glass down and wiped his frothy moustache with his coat sleeve. He had never tasted champagne quite like this before. It was smooth as ice, and slightly bitter, and the taste lingered at the back of his throat, inviting more.

"Is good," he said and belched.

Littledyke downed his drink and said, "Glad you like it. Have some more." He leaned across the table and winked heavily at Markovic. "They're paying," he said.

Markovic nodded sagely. They drank. Then, remembering

what he had come for, Markovic took out the notebook with a list of questions he had been told to ask. He opened it and wrote the date and time. Then looking up at Littledyke, he asked "What is your given name?"

"My given what?"

Markovic said, "I am Ladislav Markovic, you are what Littledyke?"

"Harry," Littledyke said.

Markovic wrote it down.

"Hey! What do you think you are doing?"

Markovic looked up from the notebook. "For my superiors."

"Sod your superiors! What do you think will happen if anyone else finds that notebook?"

Markovic shut the notebook and stared disconsolately at Littledyke. "I am sorry," he said. "I did not think."

"You're just a bleeding amateur, aren't you?"

Markovic looked down at the table. "This is first time," he admitted. "I have to make report."

Littledyke poured out another drink. "Make your report," he said. "But keep the information up here." He tapped his head.

Markovic nodded. He was leaning a lot from this first meeting. "Alright," he said, "you don't worry," and he tapped his own head. "I will remember." He cupped his hands round his glass and asked: "You work on aeroplane, yes?"

But Littledyke was looking past Markovic, a rapt expression on his face. He let out a soft sigh. "Hey! Watch that!"

"That" was a coloured girl in a leopard skin. It had been a very small leopard. She gyrated slowly under the revolving lights, skin smooth and glossy. Markovic felt his breath catch in his throat and drank more of the champagne. It would be nice, he thought, if they had a few colour problems in his own country.

55

"Those tits," Littledyke breathed heavily into Markovic's ear, "Gorgeous!"

"How you spell tits?" Markovic demanded.

Littledyke told him. "Why do you want to know?"

"I am learning English," Markovic said. "For me tits is new word." He raised his glass and swallowed. "From you, Harry, I learn much new words, yes."

"Oh sure," Littledyke said and drank.

The girl finished her act. Markovic clapped enthusiastically. Harry leaned across and said, "Let's get the business over, shall we? Then I'll ask old Nicholas to send a couple of girls over and we can have fun."

Markovic decided he wouldn't have fun. He reminded himself that Harry was a spy.

"You don't know Nicholas, do you?"

Markovic shook his head.

"He's terrific! Used to be a pilot and he's got some fabulous girls. Real you know what."

Markovic didn't. But he was always prepared to learn.

Harry Littledyke drank and said, "First, about money."

Markovic said nothing. He didn't know what to say.

"This is first-rate stuff I'm giving you, so the money's got to be good, see."

Markovic said, "You tell me about the aeroplane, yes?" He took out his notebook and laid it on the table.

Harry said, "I can't tell you about the plane yet. They haven't finished flight testing yet. But I'll get all the gen on it, don't you worry. All the specs, climb rates, dimensions, suppliers, the lot. But let's get the money out of the way first, OK?"

Markovic said, "How fast?"

Harry said, "You're pushing boy-o, you're pushing." He gulped at his drink and smiled. "But I'm glad you asked that, Ladislav. I'm beginning to like you. I have a feeling about you." He pounded his chest again. "I trust you."

Harry leaned forward and clapped Markovic on the shoulder, pulled him closer so that he could whisper. "I'll tell you what they expect," he whispered hoarsely. "Mach 2. 2." He opened his eyes wide in amazement.

Mach 2. 2 was twice the speed of sound. A fighter travelling that fast was incredible. But then, Markovic thought, these English were an incredible people. At home he had been taught that Kuzentsov had invented television and Lyulka the jet engine. Here in England, they claimed that someone called Baird had invented television and you only had to look at the BBC to realise which was which. Now, if they were making jet engines that were so powerful, could not the English have invented that too.

"That is very fast," he said.

"Right. And I'll tell you something else. There have been delays on the programme."

"Sabotage?" Markovic asked.

"No. The frogs."

"Sabotage with frogs?" Perhaps the plane could travel under water as well.

"No you don't understand. Frogs. Frenchies. It's a combined operation. Us and the Frenchies. Tell you something, Ladislav, I'd rather have one German on my side than ten Frenchmen."

"East Germans," Markovic asked, "or West?"

"The French are too soft. Too much wine and garlic and l'amour. Not the sort of people you want building aircraft. I always say, if you want a good industrial job done, take a German or take a Swede, or a Belgian or one of your own people. They work hard too. But not the flipping French."

Markovic fetched another sheet of paper from his pocket

57

and squinted at it. "What is approximate service ceiling?"

"Now, now Ladislav, you know what the Chinese say."

"We do not approve of Chairman Mao," Markovic said stiffly.

"Not him, twit. The Chinese, like in Gerrard Street, the flied lice boyos."

It was getting too much for Markovic.

"The Chinese say, no tickee, no laundry." Harry smiled. "So there you are."

Markovic wondered exactly where he was.

"No cash, no goods," Harry said softly. "You can't expect me to give it away, can you. I've given you a free sample, haven't I?"

"We fix price afterwards," Markovic said solemnly.

"What do you think I am! Some kind of bond salesman! This is really secret stuff, Ladislav. I mean you couldn't walk down the street and buy it or anything. It's real grade one classified."

"How much?" Markovic asked. He had a weird sensation of floating and was beginning to feel hot. He undid his tie.

"Two and one half," Harry said.

"Two and one half what?" Markovic asked. He thought it a good question.

"Thousand. Of course," Harry said. "Pounds."

Markovic gulped. "I'll need authorisation," he said.

"Fine," Harry said. "Get authorisation. But don't take all year about it. I can always go elsewhere, you know."

"We will pay," Markovic said.

"And there's five hundred expenses."

"No," Markovic said. "No expenses." Did Harry take him for a fool? Even in Moscow they knew about expense accounts.

"OK," Harry said. "Two and a half grand then and believe me Ladislav, that's cheap."

Markovic smiled. He leant across the table. "Two and a half grand. That's good." He smiled. He'd learnt a new word.

It was then that Harry suggested they should have one more drink, to celebrate their newfound friendship. Two drinks later they agreed that if there were more people like them, there wouldn't be any war, hot, cold or temperate.

Four drinks later, Harry spoke to his friend Nicholas and three girls came and sat with them. The coloured girl sat on Markovic's knee.

Soon after that, Markovic stopped counting.

He remembered that they had sung and everyone had applauded when he had got to the seventeenth stanza of a ballad on how difficult it was to get a tractor across the Volga. Markovic had been quite elated at the applause. No one had cheered him for singing before.

The girls had kissed him and fondled him and one of them had bitten his moustache. He had kissed them and fondled them, and bitten one on the shoulder. There had been wild and weird and wonderful music that had twisted Markovic's heart into a little ball. And the coloured girl had thighs as smooth as glass.

Sometime, much, much later a girl had climbed on the table and danced, just for him and Harry. It had been even better when she started to take off her clothes. And he had danced too. The coloured girl had called him a wild Cossack, and he had got up on the table and kicked his feet up and shouted: "Hoy! Hoy!" And tried to jump over Harry Littledyke's head.

They had picked him up and put him back on the table and the girls had said he was so agile and he had such a lovely body and he had to take his shirt off and show them, and in time his trousers had come off too.

Finally, the table had collapsed.

59

12

Nicholas Maasten stood amidst the mess of glass and shattered furniture, shaking his head slowly. He was holding a telephone at the end of a long extension cord and he was speaking most severely to Harry Littledyke. If Harry Littledyke didn't know it, he, Nicholas Maasten, ran a respectable club. He, Nicholas Maasten, didn't want any trouble, not with the neighbours and specially not with the police. Last night there had been complaints. The police had been round to see him, and one of the girls had sprained her ankle and wouldn't be able to perform for two weeks.

"Oh! Come off it, Nick," Harry said. "People don't come there to look at ankles. They can see ankles any day of the week, right. They come to see a bit of art, tits, that sort—"

"They won't be seeing Diane's," Maasten snapped. "Your drunk friend bit them."

"He didn't! Oh Jesus, I am sorry. Bet Ladislav will be sorry too—"

"He will," Maasten promised, "if he comes here and starts biting again. You're a right pair, both of you. And what about the damage?"

"They'll take care of it," Harry said.

"Sure," Maasten said. "Sure. But next time, Harry, do me a favour. Keep it quiet."

"Of course, Nicholas," Harry said indignantly. "What do you think I am!"

Maasten put the phone down and turned to the barman standing beside him. "What's the damage?" he asked.

"Eight bottles of champagne, twenty-six Guinness, one bottle Polish white spirit, two shots rum, nine nips whisky, one Tia Maria, four Canada Dry, seven Martell and eight Carlsbergs."

"Holy smoke!" Maasten exclaimed. "Did they walk out of here or did they float?"

"Neither," the barman said. "They were carried."

Maasten shook his head in mock despair. "OK. Get out a bill for the booze. And Norman—"

"Yes?"

"Invoice the champagne as Pol Roger."

"But it was non vintage, Nicholas."

Maasten grinned. "Who'd know the difference now?"

He placed a suede boot delicately amongst the wreckage. Three tables, he thought, Carruthers would be good for twenty quid each on that. Four chairs at a fiver a piece, God knew how many glasses. Maasten smiled. As long as Carruthers paid, he hoped Harry Littledyke and his lugubriously moustached friend came back every night.

He bent and poked among the wreckage till he found what he was looking for. A grey metal box, hardly bigger than a packet of cigarettes. It was dented, squashed flat, twisted over. Sod Harry Littledyke, Maasten thought. That transmitter had cost seventy-two dollars and even though Carruthers would pay one hundred dollars for it, he didn't know where he could get another one before the next time.

13

THE PHONE JANGLED, cutting through sleep like a blunt-edged knife. Amory stirred, felt Sue move naked in his arms and pulled her tight. He buried his head in the crook of her neck, taking comfort from the warm familiar feel of her.

She twisted and got an arm out. Then she was shaking him. "Darling! It's for you."

Amory turned and took the phone. Automatically he looked at the luminous face of the alarm clock by the bed. It was twenty past four. It must still be afternoon, he thought, and said, "Amory here."

"I'm sorry to disturb you," McGregor said. "What time are you seeing our friend again?"

"Six thirty," Amory replied.

"Could you make arrangements to stay with him?" McGregor asked. "All the time."

Amory grunted, "I suppose so."

McGregor said "It is necessary I'm afraid. I've had two people with him all the afternoon. He refuses to talk to anyone but you."

Amory didn't say anything. It happened sometimes. A man on the run, frightened, confused, desperately needing something to hold on to, something that gave him a sense of security. It was just his bad luck that Kiriov had picked him.

"You will have to talk to him, I'm afraid," McGregor said.

"All right," Amory said.

"We have got provisional authorisation," McGregor said, "provided we can get a reasonable sample. Do you think you can get that?"

"I'll try," Amory said.

"I've sent round some books and some records," McGregor said. "And a chess set. They all play chess, don't they?"

"I believe so," Amory said. He put the phone down.

Sue asked, "Anything wrong?"

"I've got to go away for a few days," Amory said. "That's all."

She squeezed a Benson and Hedges from the pack on the table and lit it. "You won't be back for Wednesday, I suppose."

Amory came off nights on Tuesday and they had planned to see Bogart in *Casablanca* at the NFT on Wednesday.

"I don't know," Amory said. "I don't think so. Why don't you go with Keith?"

"I'll ask him," Sue said.

Amory looked down at her and smiled. "I am sorry, darling," he said and pulled her down into the bed.

"Let me go, you great big oaf," she cried. "You'll burn the sheets."

Amory laughed and kissed her. He didn't have to be back with Kiriov for another two hours and there was time enough to make love. They came together slowly, deliciously, like it was the last time.

*   *   *

Kiriov moved the rook to Q8. "Check," he said, "mate."

Amory stared at the board. "All right," he said and picked

63

up the pieces. "You win." It was the third game he'd lost in succession that evening. He relaid the pieces and moved the white pawn to Q4.

"No, no," Kiriov cried. "You must open strong. Here I show you. I teach you Ruy Lopez." Kiriov replaced the pawn and brought the king's pawn forward. Then he moved the knight to KB3.

"It is an old opening," he said, "but very strong."

"Anatol," Amory said. "They're prepared to give you what you asked. But they want a sample."

Kiriov moved the bishop to Kt5.

"That's good," Kiriov said. He had been prepared for that request too.

*   *   *

Mick looked at them suspiciously. "You two fellows don't like chips or what?"

"We're dieting," McGregor said.

"You must be. One breakfast for two people!" Mick slapped the mugs of tea on the counter. Men in good suits were the meanest bastards, he thought, them and bloody Protestants. Together they'd be the ruination of him.

"I've eaten," McGregor said pacifically.

Mick scowled at him. "When I shout you come and get it."

They went back to the formica-top tables clutching their thick, chipped mugs of tea.

"So all he gave you were the names," McGregor said.

"He said they were part of a spy ring operating in this country. Not an important part, mind you, but an adequate sample."

McGregor looked at Amory's notes. "I had better keep these," he said. "We've got to file these with Records. Every-

64

thing has to go on file with that blasted computer. It's a new regulation."

"I'll remember it," Amory promised.

"You'll have to get more than this," McGregor said. "Especially if we are to spend thirty thousand pounds."

"I will," Amory said.

When he got back to the flat, he did precisely that.

*　　*　　*

Three hours later a black government limousine picked Amory up outside the flat and whisked him in whispering luxury down the Edgware Road and into Park Lane. Outside the Hilton, the car stopped. A few moments later a tall, ruddy-faced man came out of the hotel and climbed into the car.

"You are Amory?" he said.

Amory said, "Yes." It was the first time he had met C. He noticed the thick shoulders and the short neck. He noticed the clear blue eyes, the shaggy white hair and the urbane diplomat's expression and the narrow face.

C said, "You've done well, Amory. Quite a catch, eh?"

The car drifted down Park Lane towards Hyde Park Corner.

"Damn sorry I have to meet you like this. But it's all rush, with the P.M.'s visit to Brussels."

"I didn't know that involved us," Amory said.

"It does," C replied. "Security, you know. Have to get it right. Combined operation with the French and the Germans and the Belgians." He laughed drily. "Have to make sure that if anything goes wrong it won't be our chaps' fault." He took Amory by the arm. "Did Kiriov say anything more than the names?" he asked.

"Yes sir, he gave me more names."

65

m," he said. "You'd better tell me about it."

Amory did.

When he had finished, C said, "I suppose you'd better report directly to me. Save time, you know."

Amory said, "I'll file reports with Records, sir."

"Good heavens man, why?"

"It's a new regulation, sir. Because of the computer."

C laughed. "I forgot," he said. "I am getting off at the French Embassy," he said. "Have the car drop you off where you like."

"Thank you, sir," Amory said. "But there's something else."

"What?"

"Something about a supersonic fighter, sir."

"There's always something about a supersonic fighter," C said. "We live in the jet age."

"This one is something special, sir. No one in the Department knows anything about it."

"And Kiriov does, eh?"

Amory shook his head. "He knows how some of the information is going to be passed on to them," he said.

C coloured. "My God, Amory," he said. "This is damned serious."

14

ADRIAN QUIMPER PERCHED on the high stool in front of the oyster bar and sipped his sherry. He had agreed to meet Chubby Prendergast for lunch and as usual Chubby Prendergast was late. In that at least Chubby Prendergast hadn't changed.

The narrow room was filling up. People were being ushered through it into the restaurant on the first floor. Quimper looked at the menu and thought, eighteen varieties of sole, how fabulous, and looked at the door and saw the girl.

She was beautiful, a laughing-eyed brunette with hair that fell to her shoulders and a complexion that was golden. She was slim in the way that was fashionable nowadays, with narrow bony hips and high well-shaped breasts.

The last time Quimper had seen her she had been with Amory. They had made a good-looking couple. Now, he remembered that he hadn't seen Amory since the night he had helped get the Russian out of Tottenham Court Road police station. There were rumours in the Department that the Russian was a specially big catch. He wondered if when he met Amory, Amory would tell him about it.

The girl came into the restaurant, head turning, looking for someone.

Quimper leaned across and said, "If it's Amory you are looking for, he isn't here."

She whirled, staring at him, puzzled. Then she said, "I am not—"

Quimper smiled. "I met you with him some weeks ago, at Rules."

She said, "Oh you're Mr.—"

"Quimper, Adrian Quimper."

She laughed. "Of course, I remember. I'm sorry. You two work together, don't you?"

"That's right," Quimper said. "Would you like a drink?"

"I am looking for Keith," she said. "You haven't seen him, have you? Oh, what am I saying! You don't even know Keith."

"You might as well have that drink," Quimper said, "until Keith gets here."

"All right," she said and clambered up the stool next to him. "I'll have a Campari and soda."

Quimper watched her fingers curl round the glass, long bronzed fingers tipped in coral. It was nice, he thought, to occasionally have a drink with a beautiful girl.

"I haven't seen Amory for a couple of days," he said.

She laughed and shook her head. "Me neither."

"I suppose he is on a job, then," Quimper said.

Her face clouded. She fought it away. "Yes," she said, "playing one of your little mysterious games."

Quimper remembered that Amaryk had thought of it like that too.

The girl drank and told him about a film she had seen.

A few minutes later a tall auburn-haired man came up and kissed her on the cheek. He had enough of her good looks for Quimper to recognise a family resemblance.

"This is my brother, Keith," she said.

They shook hands and spoke desultorily. Then her brother took her away to the restaurant on the first floor and Quimper settled down to wait for Chubby Prendergast.

* * *

"Anatol," Amory said. "You've got to tell me more."

"How much more you want? Yesterday I give you names. You come back this afternoon and I give you more names. I tell you about the aeroplane. What do you want? That I tell you everything? Then what will happen to poor Kiriov when you don't need him no more?"

"They say it isn't cnough," Amory said.

"It never will be enough," Kiriov said. "They always want more. Now, tomorrow, you go back and tell them Kiriov says enough. You say Kiriov will not tell any more till he have a piece of paper signed by your government agreeing to thirty thousand pounds."

"And asylum."

Kiriov laughed. "You understand quick," he said. He got to his feet and went round to the bookcase under which the chess set was stored. "Tonight," Kiriov said, "I show you a Nizmovitch Defence."

At that moment the door bell rang.

Amory started to his feet, hand reaching underneath his jacket for the butt of the Walther. Heathcote had delivered their dinner, had eaten with them, and taken the remains away. Amory wasn't expecting any callers.

Then the bell rang again. Three times.

Amory waited. The bell rang twice.

He let the Walther slip back into its holster. It was the code.

The bell rang once more.

That was it. Probably Heathcote coming back for a chat,

69

or one of the others, not knowing the flat was occupied, bringing back a bit of skirt.

Amory opened the door and stared in surprise. "I wasn't expecting—" he began, and then he saw the pistol.

Too late he grabbed for the Walther.

The man fired. At point-blank range the bullet crashed through Amory's chest, sending him wheeling to fall on his face in the centre of the lounge.

Kiriov whirled and gave a high-pitched scream. In blind panic, he rushed at the stranger, trying to get to the door.

The man fired again. The bullet caught Kiriov in the face.

15

HERMIONE CAME INTO Maasten's cramped office, wearing a mask. She had a six-pointed gold star in her crotch and two smaller stars on each of her nipples. She was wearing a large floppy hat and nothing else. She was supposed to be the Lone Ranger.

"Nicholas," she said, "they're here. They're at number twelve."

"I know," Maasten said, adjusting the earpiece and swearing at bloody Jap earphones that were too bloody small.

"Oh! Nicky! You're listening to them! Here, give us a listen."

"Go away Hermione, I'm working."

"I don't call that working. Listening to customers' private conversations that is, that's criminal."

"Hermione," Maasten asked, "how would you like to make five quid?"

"All right," she said.

"Could you go downstairs and move the flower vase on twelve, six inches to the right." Maasten hoped they wouldn't start dancing on the tables again.

"All right," Hermione said and went. It was the easiest five quid she'd ever earned.

A crackle followed by a sharp increase in volume announced that Hermione had accomplished her mission. Harry Littledyke's voice came through, loud and clear. "Forty degrees sweep back on horizontal and forty-three degrees on vertical surfaces." His voice was accompanied by a squeaking noise. Maasten checked to see if the tape recorder spools were functioning correctly. They were. "Trailing edges with a honeycomb core." Maasten listened. The squeaking continued.

"Tyre size five hundred and fifty by two hundred and fifty point six. Pressure forty pounds per square inch."

"Harry," Markovic said. "Have you a pen. I've finished the lead in my pencil."

"Sure," Harry said. "You got all that down, Ladislav?"

"Of course, yes, Harry. It is frightful interesting. Some day I become pilot, yes."

"When we buy our island."

"Peace island," Markovic said. "Oh yes. That will be, you will like my new word Harry, splendid."

Maasten couldn't help smiling. They were as thick as thieves and nearly as drunk. He left the earphones and poured himself a drink. Then he came back and listened some more as they went through the systems and the electronics. "Decca RDN 72 doppler radar, HF/UHF radio, fully automatic inertial system with digital computer."

"Interesting," Maasten thought and began to scribble a few notes. Even more interesting, he thought, and made a few calculations. Take-off run one thousand four hundred and eighty feet, gross wing area two hundred and fifty-eight point three square feet, maximum weight thirty thousand eight hundred and sixty-five pounds.

Maasten rechecked his calculations and leaned back in his

chair. He lit another cigarette. Something, he felt, had gone horribly wrong.

But he was not supposed to monitor their conversations. He was not supposed to do anything more than provide them with a place to meet and give them enough food and drink. So Maasten decided, there was nothing he could do about it, except pray that the Department would realise, if and when they played back the tapes.

PART II

"Folks of a surly Tapster tell . . ."
Fitzgerald,
Rubaiyat of Omar Khayyam

16

THE BODIES LAY AWKWARDLY across the living room carpet, limbs twisted in angular rectitude. They were fully clothed, white, male, had been in their early thirties. Both men had been shot.

One lay on his back by the sofa, arms outflung in a despairing open rectangle. The bullet that had killed him had hit him in the face half an inch away from the left nostril. Apart from one eye drooping on its nerve ends like a globule of snot, there was not much left of the man's face.

From where he stood Adrian Quimper could see quite clearly the gaping hole left by the bullet. The flesh was like a sticky red curtain and it was topped by wispy strands of black hair. Underneath the hair he could see the silver grey underside of the brain.

Mechanically he memorised details. Blue serge suit, blue nylon shirt, striped tie trailing with the surprise of the fall. The man had been 160 pounds, about 5 feet 8 inches and the bullet had blasted its way out through the fragile curve of the forehead, spattering blood and fat and fish-like slivers of flesh over the sofa and the dowdy brown Axminster.

Soft-nosed high velocity cartridge fired at close range, Quimper surmised, stepping over the man's outstretched legs to look at the second body. It lay face down, the thatch of regulation length blond hair hardly dishevelled by the fall. An exit wound blossomed obscenely in the centre of the man's back, a mess of blood and powder and charred grey Terylene. It looked as if the impact of the bullet had spun the man round before he fell.

Gingerly Quimper lifted the stiff shoulder. The bullet had caught the man just above the heart. The carpet had pressed a gentle ribbed pattern into the softly yielding flesh of the cheeks and the eyes stared back at Quimper like glazed blue marbles.

Quimper thought of the chestnut-haired girl, remembered the coral-tipped fingers curling round the frosted glass. "Poor sod," thought Quimper, noticing that the jacket was still buttoned, that Amory hadn't even had time to get his gun out of the holster.

He thought again of the girl, remembering Amaryk, remembering the bleached white houses like dried bones in the Mediterranean sun. He reflected how easy it was to have made a mistake, to have taken a wrong turning, to have made a false gesture. He reflected how easy it was to have died simply because one had left one's jacket buttoned.

He remembered London and the mews garage in the half dark of an autumn evening, the figure cavorting between the dismembered cars, the sudden whirling turn and the dull glint of metal. Most of all he remembered the gun kicking against his own wrist, and then he came aware of Bridgenorth staring at him across the body on the carpet, eyes pressed like sultanas into the florid face.

"It's Amory," Quimper said, "one of ours."

Slowly Quimper straightened up, biting his lips at the twinge behind the knees and in the small of the back.

Bridgenorth was talking to him, mouth opening and closing

78

under the heavy moustache like a mechanical trap. Even at that hour of the morning Bridgenorth smelt of beer.

"It was Williams who answered the call," Bridgenorth was saying. "Bright lad. Thought to check who owned the flat."

The flat was on the sixth floor of an Edwardian development that managed, despite the high ceilings of the time, to give an atmosphere of boxiness. It was decorated in a drab brown that even the William Morris patterned wallpaper could do nothing for. It was lumpy, overcrowded and anonymous, one of those one bdrm. k. and b. places that was so far on the wrong side of Kilburn that it couldn't fetch more than twelve guineas a week.

The room was full of civilians. It was surprising, Quimper reflected, how many civilians were involved in police work. There were the three lab technicians dusting door knobs with powder, a medical orderly standing uselessly by the door and the photographer waiting impatiently for them to move, the large Rollei and umbrella flash threatening to pull his scrawny head off his shoulders.

Quimper said: "This will have to be kept quiet."

"We have a job to do," Superintendent Bridgenorth said.

Quimper looked at him levelly. "Yes," he said. "We all do."

Bridgenorth led the way to the bedroom. "It was the cleaning lady who found them. I've kept her here, in case."

"Thanks," Quimper said matter of factly. "I can get authorisation you know. D Notices and that."

Superintendent Bridgenorth turned, beefy hand on the door. They both knew that D Notices involved the Home Secretary. "That won't be necessary," Bridgenorth said. Then as if afraid of conceding defeat too rapidly, "Not for a few days."

"Till the inquest," Quimper said, obliging.

79

Bridgenorth opened the door. "Mrs. Holmes," he said. "This is Detective —" he hesitated, "this is Adrian Quimper. He wants to ask you some questions."

Mrs. Holmes gave a sob and twisted the denim bag on her lap even tighter. She was a small buxom woman with faded brown hair and faded button eyes. She was wearing a vivid check overcoat with a large tortoiseshell brooch on the lapel. Her head was still bound in a paisley scarf. "It was horrible," she muttered, "horrible. Finding them like that."

Quimper pulled the stool from in front of the dressing table and sat down opposite Mrs. Holmes. The room was like the rest of the flat, brown and dowdy. The high double bed filled most of it, dwarfing the dressing table and heavy clumsy wardrobe. Watery morning light meandered through the uncurtained window.

"You clean here regularly?" Quimper asked.

Mrs. Holmes nodded and began to sob again. Quimper watched the broken nailed hands twist round the handle of the denim bag. The fingers were short and stubby, the nails washed pale.

"Thursdays," Mrs. Holmes sobbed. "Thursdays. The same day I do the Hendlesohns'."

"What time do you get to the Hendlesohns'?"

"Mrs. Hendlesohn likes me to be there by half past eight so she can take the children to school. I take a number 16 from here. Right to the door."

Quimper looked at the WPC standing by the bed, thick-legged in flat-heeled shoes. "I think Mrs. Holmes would like a cigarette," he said.

Mrs. Holmes smoked the cigarette greedily. Her eyes were rimmed with red and there was a tiny network of purple veins about the end of her nose.

"How long have you been cleaning this flat?" Quimper asked.

"Six, seven months."

"Who hired you?"

"The owner. He said he would be away quite a lot and that sometimes there would be friends to stay and that it was all right and I was to come every Thursday regular. I was to clean up and my wages would be kept on the mantelpiece."

For the first time she looked directly at Quimper. "Three pounds a week it was and one pound Christmas box."

"When did you last see the owner?"

"Not since that day. He's been away. Travelling."

"Yes," Quimper said, "What time did you come here today?"

"The usual time. Six thirty. The lift isn't working then. They usually stop it at two in the morning, so I came up the stairs. It's a long climb at my age so I usually stop on three for a breather."

"And today? Did you stop at three?"

"Yes," Mrs. Holmes said, "I stopped at three. Today I felt that something terrible was going to happen." She began to cry again.

"So what time did you enter the flat?"

"I don't know," she sobbed, "soon after six thirty."

"And then what happened? Tell me."

Mrs. Holmes wiped her eyes with the back of her wrist and took a long drag at the cigarette. "The door was on the latch," she said.

"Was that unusual?"

Mrs. Holmes hesitated. Quimper beckoned to the WPC to give her another cigarette.

"No," she said. "The door had been on the latch before." She paused and wriggled slightly on the bed as if trying to make herself more comfortable. "Sometimes there used to be young ladies here."

"Oh," Quimper said. "I see." Quimper thought of the girl he had seen with Amory. Had she stayed here? Here amongst the drab brown furniture and the steady thrum of traffic had she and Amory found peace?

Mentally he began to draft a memorandum reminding staff that staff houses were not to be used for casual sexual encounters. Quimper too had his job to do.

"So today I thought he would be here."

"Who?"

"The blond one." She closed her eyes and pointed to the door. "Out there."

"Go on, Mrs. Holmes."

"A very light sleeper he was. He'd hear me coming into the flat and always he used to put his head round the bedroom door." Mrs. Holmes began to cry again. "'Ada,'" he would say, "'make us a nice cuppa will you. Ever so charming he was. If he was alone sometimes we'd have a right old natter."

"And today?" Quimper asked.

"My name isn't Ada," Mrs. Holmes said dabbing at her eyes with a handkerchief. "It's Mary."

"And today the door was on the latch?"

"I thought nothing of it," Mrs. Holmes said, "till I saw . . ." Her face broke again and the WPC reached out and patted her soothingly on the shoulder.

"What did you do then, Mrs. Holmes?"

"I screamed and ran out of the flat. There was someone on the landing of five, going to work. He took me into his flat and he called the police."

"Mrs. Holmes, this morning, did you see anyone in the building when you came up the stairs? Anyone at all? Please think carefully."

Mrs. Holmes thought carefully. "Only the man on five," she said with a small voice.

"And the flat? Did you see anyone going into or leaving it?"

She shuddered, "No," she said. "No one."

Quimper stood up. "Thank you Mrs. Holmes," he said, "you have been most helpful." He looked across to Superintendent Bridgenorth. "We'll have a police car take you round to the Hendlesohns'."

"No," Mrs. Holmes whispered, "it's too late now. She would have gone with the children. Besides, she wouldn't like me coming there in a police car. Mrs. Hendlesohn is a very proper person."

Quimper smiled thinly. "Then we'll have you taken home," he said. "In a car without a blue light."

*   *   *

A flash bulb flared like summer lightning. The photographer moved round squatting low to get a better angle. A man stood in the centre of the room clutching a black bag and smiling humourlessly. There were more civilians in the room now, measuring, dusting, scraping threads of tobacco from the ashtrays. Someone had drawn the blind and the pale light of a summer that had come too late flooded the room.

Quimper turned to Bridgenorth. "What about the neighbours? Anyone see or hear anything?"

"My people are talking to them."

"I'd like to know as soon as possible."

Bridgenorth smiled: "I'll be in touch. We have to co-operate, you know."

They walked past the bodies. Amory had been turned round so that he lay on his back. "The other one," Bridgenorth said, "name of Anatol Kiriov. Foreigner."

Quimper stopped, heart racing momentarily. Then he forced himself to walk slowly towards the door, proceeding,

83

as they called it when he'd been on the beat, in an orderly manner.

"Must be Russian," he said.

"Who'll tell them?" Bridgenorth asked.

"You will," Quimper said. "In time."

The constable outside the door saluted as they stepped into the narrow carpeted corridor. The walls were pressed close together like the gangways on a ship. Quimper walked to the lift aware of Bridgenorth following massively behind him.

"He must have used a shotgun," Bridgenorth said. "We'll start looking for that."

Quimper shook his head. No professional killer would risk walking up six flights of stairs carrying a weapon that was difficult to conceal and cumbersome to use in a confined space. Besides Quimper had seen wounds like that before and they hadn't been caused by a shotgun. "I'd look for something smaller," he said, "a Luger or a Mauser."

"But they're only pistols."

Quimper stopped in front of the lift and turned to face Bridgenorth. "What you do," he said, "is crimp the soft nose of the slug. That ensures maximum damage."

"Oh," Bridgenorth said. "Really."

"It's outlawed by the Geneva Convention," Quimper said and jabbed the lift button. The doors whirred open and he stepped inside.

"If he used a pistol," Bridgenorth said, "it must have been someone they knew well. To let him get that close, I mean."

Quimper looked at him expressionlessly. "Who would they both know?" he asked.

*   *   *

Quimper hurried down the crescent driveway and along the pavement to where his Rover was parked. The air was damp and a chilling breeze cut between the narrow buildings. Quimper sighed. It was that kind of summer.

He climbed into the car and leaned against the worn leather seat. For a moment he sat still listening to the steady rumble of traffic pouring greedily towards the West End. A train flashed across Kilburn Bridge, breaking out of the dark night of the underground.

Quimper started up the car and edged gently into the stream of traffic. He drove slowly to the office, savouring the mild sunshine, savouring the last moment of peace. He knew that by the time he got to Bedford Square, all hell would have broken loose.

17

BY THE TIME QUIMPER GOT BACK to the office hell had broken loose, but in a superbly controlled way.

"There's a flap on," Vivian Ingleby cried. "The Super wants to see you at eleven. Ack Emma."

Quimper grimaced. When he had returned to the Department four years previously, Vivian Ingleby had been passed on to him, with a mixture of gratitude and relief. She was ten years younger than Quimper, a trim compact woman, with bronzed freckled skin and large hands. She had worked for MI5 at a time when recruitment was based upon a Roedean education, good legs and an ability to ride horses. The legs were thicker now but still good, and as, since joining the Department she'd had little cause to ride horses, the rest of her remained commendably firm.

"Carruthers wants to see you," she said, "*before* you go in to the Super."

"What for?"

"He didn't say."

Quimper shrugged. Vivian's small room smelt richly of Blue Mountain which she bought herself and brewed in a heavy metal percolator. A calendar, the gift of some grocer in Brighton, hung on one wall and below that was the battered

86

IBM typewriter. Vivian had typed "The quick brown fox jumped over the lazy dog" seventeen times. It was what she called limbering up. Quimper was never sure who or what was being limbered.

Quimper said : "Could you come into my office and take down a report."

His office was twice as big as Vivian's cubicle and decorated in the standard green and cream. His compact Design Council desk stood in the centre of the room, an edge of black hessian carpet peeking hesitantly round it.

The size of the carpet was a direct measure of Quimper's importance to the Department. Normally section heads were entitled to carpets covering the centre of the room. But Security didn't rate that kind of expenditure. It didn't even rate more than two visitors' chairs without arms.

Except, Quimper thought, today.

Until today Quimper's duties had been routine. Vetting new staff was perhaps the most time-consuming. Besides that he checked registers of inward and outward mail, completed the duty rosters, ensured that the numerous keys were properly signed for and made certain that any drawing of arms or ammunition was properly authorised. Until today it had been dull undemanding work, it had been an ideal prelude to retirement.

Early this morning, Amory had been killed. It was the first time since Quimper had rejoined the Department that an operative had been killed on home territory. And that made it his responsibility.

Quimper felt the old excitement flow through him. It was like the time when he had first joined the police, when he had made seventy-six arrests in one year and had been on the verge of becoming the youngest detective inspector in the Metropolitan Police. It was like the time he had first worked

87

for the Department. Exciting, and for the first time in years, useful.

A strong smell of coffee wafted under his nostrils. He came aware of Vivian standing in front of him, a trifle mannish in an open-necked blue shirt. "You still want to dictate? Or shall I come back after dreamy-time?"

"No," Quimper said, "Stay." With an effort he collected his thoughts and began to dictate a report of the morning's events.

"How many copies?" Vivian asked.

"One plus three."

"Who is the extra copy for?" Normally, McGregor got a copy of every report and a second copy went down to Mr. Pute of Records for processing on his computer.

Quimper said: "The third copy is for Carruthers. Amory was R Section."

Vivian scribbled busily, head bent over her pad, crossing round knees under the too tight skirt.

"Poor Amory," she said when Quimper had finished. "Did he have a family?"

"No," Quimper said, thinking of the girl he'd seen with Amory at Rules. "Not what you'd call family."

She snapped her pad shut. "Is that all?"

"No," Quimper said, "I have to do a memorandum. *'To Section Head R. It has been brought to our notice that operatives have been using departmental accommodation for non-business activities. All operatives are reminded that this constitutes a grievous breach of security and that offenders will be severely dealt with.' Private to Carruthers. 'Please ensure that all members of your section read this.'* Got that?"

Vivian raised her head. Ringlets of grey mingling with the tight brunette curls glinted in the light. "Yes," she said. Then: "That sounds terrific! What will you do with the offenders?"

88

Quimper frowned. "They have been warned," he said at last.

He watched Vivian walk to the door, heels tapping the lino busily, charcoal-grey skirt flouncing. Her figure was still good, Quimper thought. Unkind rumours suggested that she kept it that way by playing cricket on Sundays.

"Oh, Quimper!" Vivian stopped by the door and turned. "There was a dreadfully common sort of person telephoning for you. Name of Bridgenorth."

Quimper sighed. "Detective Superintendent Bridgenorth?"

"I wouldn't know. He sounded like a lavatory cleaner. He called me 'luv'." She opened the door, went out and then thrust the tight curled head round the door. "It is now twenty-two minutes to Super-time," she cried and pulled the door shut after her.

Quimper sighed. It really would have been kinder if the Department had provided him with a talking clock.

18

QUIMPER ARRIVED IN MCGREGOR'S OFFICE, on the first floor of the Department building, at precisely eleven o'clock.

Unlike Quimper's, McGregor's office had a fitted carpet and luxuriously scattered over this were four Pakistani rugs. There was a low couch against one wall. It had a teak frame and a cane base. The headroll and legs were ornately carved and it looked as if it would be more at home on a sun-baked Indian verandah. McGregor had a fine desk with a green leather top. He also had armchairs for his visitors. A large and somewhat improbable battle scene dominated the wall opposite the couch and underneath the painting was a marble fireplace in which a gas fire glowed, set low.

The deputy head of the Department, Angus McGregor was a big man. He stood at least six-feet-two in his patterned socks and he had the thick-muscled solid body of a navvy. His face was as flat as the business end of a spade and some of this flatness lent itself to his eyes, which were blue and turned slightly upward at the corners, giving him a faintly Chinese appearance. He had a choleric complexion that matched the shock of unruly red hair that rose from his forehead like a field of unkempt corn. There were brown blotches on the backs of his hands, a souvenir of his years of service in India.

Four years ago it had been McGregor who had persuaded Quimper to return to the Department. Not that Quimper had required much persuasion. There weren't many vacancies for ex-policemen of forty-two, especially if it was rumoured that they had been taking bribes.

The job McGregor had offered required no special qualifications. Anyone with training in Security could have done it, and heaven knew, there were enough of them around. Quimper appreciated that there had been something personal in the offer, and at the time he had been reassured, grateful that someone like McGregor believed in him, despite the rumours and despite that other time in Beirut. It was almost as if, Quimper thought, he was being given a second chance.

"Morning," Quimper said, entering the room. Not for him the easy familiarity of Angus, and McGregor hated being addressed as "sir".

McGregor waved from behind the desk and Quimper turned to the other man in the room. He felt no affection at all for David Carruthers.

Carruthers said: "I thought you were seeing me first."

Quimper said: "Sorry David. It's been that kind of day."

Carruthers nodded curtly. He was a slim, tightly built man in a lightweight brown suit. He had pale, translucent eyes, a big jaw and firm thin lips. Carruthers rarely smiled.

McGregor said: "Sherry? It's only cream I'm afraid There have been difficulties in supply."

Quimper accepted the sherry. He never ceased to admire the self-possession of men like McGregor, a self-possession that never deserted them even in the gravest of crises. As his father would have said, it was to do with breeding and education and class. It had to do with a sense of moral certitude and a conviction that God had undeniably been to Eton, but that was only Quimper's opinion.

"Well, Adrian, you know I hate reports. Tell us what you have found out." McGregor was standing sideways by the window, seeming to look out over the square and into the room at Quimper at the same time.

Quimper put down his drink and reached for his notebook. It contained the outline of his report and in a monotonous voice he began to read: "I was awakened this morning at seven forty-five a.m. by a telephone call from Detective Superintendent Bridgenorth of New Scotland Yard."

"For Christ's sake!" Carruthers burst out. "You aren't in court, man, just give us the facts."

Quimper's tone did not alter. There was a right way and a wrong way to give facts. "Superintendent Bridgenorth informed me that he was at 64 Fortescue Towers, N.W.6 and that two men had been shot and killed at that address. 64 Fortescue Towers, N.W.6 is a flat leased by this Department." He paused and looked directly at Carruthers. "The flat is on the sixth floor," he said. "All the flats on that floor have a number beginning with 6."

"Go on," Carruthers said tersely.

"I proceeded immediately to the flat, arriving there at eight thirty a.m. I viewed the bodies and identified one of the deceased as Gordon Amory, known to me as an operative of R Section of this Department. I thereupon informed Detective Superintendent Bridgenorth that the Department had an interest in this matter and requested co-operation and discretion."

"Did Bridgenorth respond?" It was McGregor.

"Detective Superintendent Bridgenorth agreed to co-operate. I then interviewed a Mrs. Mary Holmes, cleaning lady, who had found the bodies approximately two hours previously. She was unable to give any information pertaining to the identification or apprehension of the assailant. Detective

Superintendent Bridgenorth informed me that he had reason to suppose that the other body in the flat was that of one Anatol Kiriov, a clerk in the Russian Trade Mission."

McGregor asked : "Reason to suppose?"

"The deceased's face had been shot away, and the body was not capable of normal identification. Detective Superintendent Bridgenorth had based his identification on an examination of the deceased's personal effects which consisted of one soiled handkerchief, a wallet containing forty-two pounds, and a letter addressed to Anatol Kiriov. There was also a Russian passport in the same name, and a receipt for a forged British passport in the name of Wilson."

"Yes," McGregor said. "And a good forgery it was too. What did you do next?"

"I returned to my office and at ten thirty-five telephoned Detective Superintendent Bridgenorth. He informed me that from a preliminary examination of the bodies, the pathologist estimated death to have occurred between seven p.m. and nine p.m. last night. Police officers have questioned the occupants of all the flats on the fifth and sixth floors of Fortescue Towers. No one admits to hearing the sound of shots or seeing anything unusual."

Quimper shut his notebook. He went on : "Last night there were two television programmes, 'The Virginian' on BBC and 'Bonanza' on ITV. Gun shots between seven and nine would not have been extraordinary."

Carruthers said : "Shall we take the jokes as read, Adrian? I suppose at that time of the evening there would have been considerable movement around the flats — visitors and so forth."

"Yes," Quimper said, wishing he had thought of that. "I suppose so."

McGregor asked, "What about the murder weapon? Has that been found yet?"

"No."

Carruthers said, "I wonder what they used."

McGregor said, "Some kind of pump gun, I expect. With a sawn-off barrel."

"The police believe it was a 9 mm Browning Hi-power pistol," Quimper said.

"The killer used hand-loaded jacketed ammunition with the nose of the bullet hollowed."

McGregor said, "Good God! Dum-dums."

Quimper said, "The Browning is standard British Army issue."

Carruthers said, "So what? It was used by everyone in the last war."

Quimper turned to McGregor. "Superintendent Bridgenorth was of the opinion that the deceased were shot by someone they both knew. The shots, you see, were fired at close range."

"But that's impossible!" Carruthers burst out.

"Except," McGregor said, "Kiriov might have been followed."

"Amory would hardly have let a KGB man into the flat. It had to be someone he knew."

"Or someone Kiriov knew," McGregor insisted. He walked to the centre of the room and stood by the desk, big hands thrust deep into his pockets. After a while he asked, "What is Bridgenorth doing about all this?"

"For the present he is treating it as a routine murder case. His men are questioning people, obtaining medical and ballistic evidence. They are investigating the matter."

"And you, Adrian?" Carruthers asked softly. "What about you?"

Quimper smiled thinly. "I am helping the police with

their inquiries." He turned to McGregor. "I think it only fair to let Detective Superintendent Bridgenorth finish his investigation, before getting directly involved."

"No," McGregor said.

"I am sorry," Quimper said. "I don't understand."

"There is no point in getting involved, Adrian," McGregor said. "In fact I doubt if Bridgenorth will ever complete his investigation. Let's look at the facts. A complete stranger walks into a flat in Kilburn and shoots two men. No one sees him coming or going, no one knows anything about him. If our 'friends' are running true to form, the man will be someone brought in specially. By now he will be back in Moscow or East Berlin or Prague or wherever he came from. No, Adrian, I don't think Bridgenorth will find anything at all. Or you."

McGregor sat down behind the desk and waited until the others were all seated. He pulled out a shiny leather case that looked as though it contained duelling pistols and from this he took out a sand blasted Dunhill. He began to fill it from a tobacco jar on the desk. "You both know the significance of Kiriov?"

Quimper said: "I was present when Amory picked him up. That's all I know."

McGregor lit his pipe. When it was drawing easily he asked: "You know that Kiriov wanted asylum?"

"I gathered there was something like that."

"Amory saw Kiriov last Saturday night. As you know, Kiriov was very drunk. Amory couldn't get much sense out of him, apart from the fact that he wanted asylum and thirty thousand pounds." McGregor nodded. "Yes, Kiriov was that important."

He got his pipe going and said, "He promised Amory that he would give him all the information on a spy ring operating

95

in this country. He promised Amory all the details when we met his conditions."

"Which were asylum and thirty thousand pounds," Quimper said.

"That's right." McGregor drew at his pipe. "There was always the possibility that Kiriov was a lunatic or more seriously, a plant. I spoke to C, and we decided to take a chance on that. We obtained permission and approval to meet Kiriov's demands, provided we had a reasonable sample of the information he had. Amory undertook to get that."

McGregor studied his pipe, raised it to his mouth and drew at it again. "Kiriov talked. He gave us names and addresses, descriptions and meeting places, safe houses and drops. But Kiriov was no fool. He had time to think everything out clearly and he knew that his only value to us was the information he brought with him. Kiriov told Amory a lot."

"But not enough," Carruthers said.

"Well," McGregor said, "I don't know. Kiriov had counted on being asked to provide a sample. So the information he gave Amory was verifiable but deliberately unrelated. The information didn't fit."

McGregor's smile broadened. "There was one thing that Kiriov didn't know. Kiriov didn't know of our Mr. Pute." McGregor leaned back in his chair and waved a deprecating hand. "I know," he said, "I've often been unkind about our Mr. Pute and his infernal computers. I resent the fact that we have to copy him on everything. I resent the fact that he and his infernal machines occupy our entire basement. I resent the fact that while we need money for so much, we've had to spend nearly fifty thousand pounds on that damned computer."

Quimper looked down, half smiling. McGregor's views on computers were well known in the Department.

96

"I've always hated the damned machines," McGregor was saying. "I've always had a big brother feeling about them. Haven't you?"

"Yes," Quimper said, "look what they have done to the banks."

McGregor stopped smiling and said, "Yes." He shifted in his chair and said: "This time, Mr. Pute proved that the fifty thousand pounds was well spent. By some devious, magical process, Mr. Pute was able to take the unrelated facts that Kiriov had given and from them build up a total file. You know, computers are wonderful things. Apparently you need only give them a little bit of information, like say David's home address, and from that the computer can relate it to other facts, whether David has a mortgage or not, who David's bankers are, his financial standing, where he works, what clubs he frequents, possibly even extract his service record. It's tremendous!" McGregor finished.

"Frightening," Quimper said.

"This time it was tremendous. Pute compiled an enormous report based on the information Kiriov had given. He has, as you know, access to the CRO computer. A kind of sexless marriage. And now, he has the report, as he says, on tape. It appears that we have a lot of information that we didn't even know we had."

"Remarkable," Quimper said.

McGregor tapped his pipe out on the raised central dome of his ashtray. He said, "Now if you gentlemen will bear with me, I will ask the infallible Mr. Pute to provide us with what he calls a 'printout' of the Kiriov report."

McGregor switched on his intercom and spoke to Records.

"Another sherry, gentlemen. Mr. Pute will be about five minutes."

Twenty minutes later Mr. Pute had not arrived. When he

97

did come he looked harassed. His lanky hair was tousled, his suit of IBM blue rumpled, and his pale blue eyes were very worried.

"Pute," McGregor cried, "what kept you? Ah, don't tell me, you know the information was classified C only and you were getting authorisation to downgrade it to section heads."

"No, sir," Pute said in a small voice, "it wasn't that."

McGregor smiled nastily. "I should have told you, I spoke to C this morning and we now have a restricted classification on the Kiriov file. David, Adrian and myself now have access." He gestured to the telephone. "Do you want to call C?"

Pute swallowed and said, "No, sir, it isn't that."

"Then what, Pute?"

"Sir," Pute said, "the tapes are missing."

19

THEY TOOK THE SERVICE LIFT at the side of the building, travelling fast downwards, surrounded by harsh-lit grey-green metal walls, like the inside of a filing cabinet. Pute was nervous, talking, gesturing delicately with pale white hands. The tapes had been classified, Top Secret, Code O, for the eyes of C only. They had been kept in the safe in his office, and now they were gone.

"Who has the keys to the safe?" Quimper asked, logical, basic, eliminating uncertainties.

"The keys. Oh. There's one in Records — in my office. I believe C has one, and McGregor."

Quimper noted the uncertainty. They had not consulted him about security when the computer was installed. That had been a job for the experts, the technocrats, men with knowledge of science and management.

"Where is the key kept?"

"Oh. In one of the drawers of my desk. Sometimes we need constant access to the safe."

"I see," Quimper said. That was only to be expected when management experts took charge of security.

"But the key isn't important. I mean, you can't open the safe with the key alone. You need the combination."

Quimper stared at Pute. Somehow the lanky frame looked clammy and soft, the face shiny under the garish lighting.

"The combination is changed every week," Pute said. "Only four of us know it. C, McGregor, my assistant and myself."

The lift braked for the basement with a force that made them bend at the knees.

Quimper asked: "What was this week's combination?"

The doors whirred open and clunked to a stop.

"Kiriov," Pute said, waiting for Quimper to step out of the lift.

Quimper repeated: "Kiriov."

"It was easy to remember," Pute said defensively as they stepped out of the lift together.

They came out of the lift into a small lobby, barred across its length by a large counter, behind which sat a uniformed guard.

"I'll have to sign you in," Pute said apologetically bending over the desk, scribbling into a book. He picked up a sticky badge and fixed it on to Quimper's jacket. "It's regulations."

The guard pressed a switch and part of the counter swung away to give them access to the steel-shuttered door. Pute inserted another card into a slot by the wall and the door slid open smoothly on hydraulic castors.

Beyond the door spotless flooring gleamed under flat, even lighting that softened away all shadows. Machines gleamed on the polished flooring, pale grey and gentle blue, somehow cold and purposeful, shaped into flowing curves. The blue overalled people moving silently between the machines looked unreal. The air was chill, sterilised, hitting the lungs with a synthetic mountain freshness. Quimper remembered Vivian telling him how easily a computer could be sabotaged by blasting smoke through the air-conditioning unit.

They went across the machine room to the row of small offices, white plywood and glass partitioning. Pute's room was slightly larger than the others. It was neat, spare, with angular metal furniture and locked filing cabinets. The walls were bare of all ornament. Only the safe behind the desk was open.

Quimper walked carefully up to the safe and squatted down, peering inside, being careful not to touch anything. The safe was empty. There was no doubt about that. "Is there another office we could use?"

Pute started with surprise. "Yes. Next door. We could use my assistant's room."

The assistant's office was identical to Pute's, except that it was smaller, and had no safe. It had the same air of ordered functionalism, the same neat sparseness. There was nothing about it that betrayed the personality of its occupier, no pictures, no packets of half-eaten sweets, no souvenirs or diplomas on the walls. There was only a notice on the door which said : *"V. V. Kumar Assistant Programme Controller."*

Quimper sat down behind the desk. "I am going to get some fingerprint men down here," he said.

Pute hesitated. "What about the operators? They'll know something's wrong." He hesitated again, "I think — don't you think — this had better be kept quiet."

"Yes," Quimper replied. "You can pass the fingerprint men off as engineers."

Quimper picked up the phone, got a direct line and spoke quickly to Bridgenorth. Then he asked Vivian to get out all the ID cards of the computer personnel.

The ID cards had been Carruthers's idea. Photographs of each employee of the Department, a brief, typed physical description and a complete set of fingerprints. None of the Department's employees had ever protested at being treated like a criminal. Security after all took precedence over privacy.

Pute asked : "You think it was someone here?"

"Maybe, maybe not. Let's wait and see what the fingerprint experts have to tell us."

Pute sat down opposite Quimper.

Quimper said : "You'd better tell me about the Kiriov tapes."

*   *   *

Pute stretched his lanky body against the metal frame of the chair, looking as if he were being spread out on a medieval torture rack.

"I programmed it," he said.

"Programmed?"

"Five days ago. After I saw Amory. I programmed the Kiriov report."

"You saw Amory? Here?"

Pute nodded. "Kiriov was Code O. Top Secret. As little as possible was committed to writing. Soon after he had seen C, Amory came down here. He gave me names, addresses, that kind of thing. I had to use that as a base and build from there."

"Did you take notes?"

"Yes. But they were destroyed after I'd done the programme."

"You'll have to tell me what a programme is."

"In simple terms, it is a set of instructions, in computer language. It tells the computer what to do. In this case the computer had to bring together all the people it knew about who were in any way associated with the people Amory had told me about."

"And what about the programme. Can't you re-run it?"

Pute looked apologetic. "It was kept with the tapes. For security."

Quimper picked up a pen and revolved it in his hand, watching the light dart off the silver cap. "Did anyone else work on the report?"

"Yes. It was quite a long job. We had to process every single tape. My assistant helped out."

"Mr. Kumar?"

Pute nodded.

"Indian?"

"He's lived in this country for years. He's got British citizenship."

Indians were normally more patriotic than that, Quimper thought. If Kumar had been in the country for a number of years, he would have no problem remaining or working. The change of citizenship must have sprung from something far deeper. If a man could change his country once, could he not do so again?

"Who else worked on the report?"

"My chief operator, Alistair Hetherset."

Quimper remembered the name. He had vetted Hetherset, when was it, three years ago? The Hethersets had lived near the school. There was an older brother, Michael. He remembered now, Michael had been killed in Malaya. And the father, a Navy officer of some kind, Commander Hetherset.

"Commander Hetherset's son?"

Pute nodded.

"Tell me, Mr. Pute, do you remember anything of the Kiriov report?"

"Some." Pute looked ashamed. "Not enough. It was mainly names and addresses, you see. Now I can see that it was important. Then really it was a matter of routine. Pure routine, converting names to numbers. That's what it's all about."

"What about the others? Would they remember?"

"Kumar only did a section. Hetherset was merely the operator." Pute hesitated. "Usually we separate programming from operating."

"For security?" Quimper asked.

"Yes. The operator only sees that the programme functions correctly. He does not have to know what the programme is about, or its purpose."

"Where is Mr. Kumar?"

"He went home about six hours ago. He's probably there, sleeping." Pute explained that Records worked a twenty-four-hour day. They rotated in three eight-hour shifts, six in the morning to two in the afternoon, two in the afternoon to ten in the evening, and from ten until six o'clock the following morning.

"Where's Hetherset?"

"He's on holiday."

"Do you know where?"

"I don't know. I think he was going abroad. He was leaving yesterday."

"I'd like to talk to him." Quimper said. "Just to talk. I know his family quite well."

Pute remained silent.

Quimper called Vivian again and got a description of Hetherset from his ID card. Then he called Bridgenorth, and asked for a port alert. "He was supposed to have left yesterday. It's only a normal check. Just delay him until one of our chaps can talk to him." Quimper paused and made a joke. "Unless, of course, he's carrying a spool of tape."

"What kind of tape?"

"A large reel of recording tape. About the size of a can of film."

"Fine," Bridgenorth said. "Like a can of film."

Before Quimper put the phone down the intercom buzzed and Pute went outside to admit the fingerprint men.

20

THERE WERE TWO OF THEM, wearing expressions of patient amiability. The tall one had a polaroid camera and flash gun, slung around his neck, while his companion clasped a battered leather case with graphite-edged fingers.

"Quimper," the taller man said.

Quimper nodded. He opened the door to Pute's office. "In there."

Both men wore sports jackets under blue gaberdine macs. Their hair was neatly cropped and they wore heavy black shoes, with toe caps. They didn't in the slightest resemble typewriter mechanics.

The man with the case looked at the safe and let out a low whistle. "Got away with much, then?"

"Enough," Quimper said.

"Neat job," the man said, "no jelly." He laid the battered leather case on the carpet. "We report to you?"

"That's right." Quimper watched the man lay his equipment out neatly beside the case and told himself there was no point in getting excited, that this was just a one-off job and he was only a retired detective inspector doing police work by accident. In any case there was nothing to get excited about. He didn't really believe the fingerprints would provide anything conclusive, but then Quimper knew that the only certain thing about investigations was that you never knew what would turn up.

He said : "I want you to do the safe and the desk."

"What about check prints?"

"Later." He waited while the man began dusting a mixture of chalk and mercury powder on to the desk. The photographer took out an exposure meter and started checking light levels. It really was like old times, Quimper thought, feeling the familiar sensation of unknowingness that accompanied the beginning of every inquiry.

"If you want me, I'll be in the next office," Quimper said and went back to Kumar's office.

Pute was standing in the middle of the room, looking as if the slightest sound would make him bolt like a gazelle.

"Sit down, Mr. Pute," Quimper said, thinking that while he waited for the fingerprint men to finish, he might as well learn something about computers.

*　　*　　*

Pute lived for computers. As he began to talk about them, his nervousness gradually disappeared, the pale hands ceased to flutter, a new authority entered his voice. Because he had his own private card system, Quimper knew that Pute had been twelve years with IBM, that he had then lectured in various American business schools for seven years before returning to England to spend another seven years with the O & M Division of Her Majesty's government.

There was no doubt that Henry Pute knew all about computers. What was even better, he could talk about them with the simplicity of the real expert. Even Quimper, who didn't quite follow the principle of the electric fuse, understood.

Down in the basement of the Department building, Records were busy converting personal data on thousands of files into mathematical symbols, a weird shorthand that compressed a man's life into a series of holes on a pink card, seven inches long and three inches wide.

"It's all," Pute said, "a matter of classification."

He took Quimper into the operations room and showed him how the cards were punched on a machine that looked like a large typewriter built into a desk. Instead of the normal typewriter carriage though, there was a large rectangular slot into which the cards were fed. The accuracy of the punched cards was then checked in a verifier, a device that looked to Quimper like a combination of a roll-top desk and a yogi's bed of nails. The verified card was finally passed through the central processing unit — the computer. This was, Pute explained, one of the smaller computers, an IBM 1130. Quimper stared at a large desk of grey and green whose surface was covered with keys, and above which lights kept flashing continuously.

The computer converted the holes on the card into magnetic impulses imprinted on large reels of tape. Each file was transferred in strict alphabetical order, and allotted a certain amount of space on the tape. By using an appropriate programme it was possible to transfer selected information from one tape to another, to have a machine like a teletype print-out this information in a series of telegram-like abbreviations.

"I could," Pute said, "provide you with the names of everyone on our files who was born in December 1937 and had been to Eton." For the first time that morning Pute smiled. "Or Pentonville."

"Remarkable," Quimper said.

"With Kiriov," Pute continued, "we had to check the information Amory gave us against everything in all the files

108

on our tapes. All the positively identified files were then transferred on to a separate tape and printed out, forming a fresh report. This is why everything took so long."

"How long would it take," Quimper asked, "to print out the information on say my file?"

Pute was almost boyish in his anxiety to please. "Not long. Not long. Why don't you go and have some coffee. There's a machine just outside the locker room."

Quimper shook his head. Vivian's Blue Mountain had spoilt machine coffee for him, for ever. "Don't let me stop you, though," Quimper said.

Pute smiled again. "I don't drink coffee," he said, "or tea."

Quimper looked at him sharply. Perhaps the man had an obscure kidney complaint. "Why?"

"It's my religion," Pute said comfortably. "I'm a Mormon, have been for years, ever since my first visit to America."

"Interesting," Quimper said and meant it. It was even more interesting that the information on Pute's religion had not appeared on Quimper's record card.

"Why don't you go into Kumar's office and sit down?" Pute suggested, selecting a tape from a rack and fitting it on to a vacant tape drive. "I'll only be a few minutes."

"Minutes?" Quimper said, "I thought computers worked faster than that."

"Oh they do. They do. In fact they operate so fast we've had to invent a new unit of time for them. The millisecond. It's us humans who cause the delay."

Quimper tried to imagine a millisecond. "I suppose it's like the Concorde," he said.

21

IN LESS THAN FIVE MINUTES Pute was back. Already Quimper was regretting the impulse that had made him ask to see his file. Graves after all were not intended to be opened.

"Shouldn't all this be confidential?" Quimper asked.

Pute shrugged. "This is purely routine information," he said. "It's restricted to Department Heads. Anything that is to do with operations is classified." Pute sat down trailing the flimsy roll of paper that contained Quimper's life evenly printed in block letters. "Adrian Russell Quimper," he read, "born Portreath, Cornwall, July 7th 1926. Parents George Russell Quimper and Marie Ellenor—"

"I know all that," Quimper said quickly. He felt nervous and embarrassed, as if being stripped naked before strangers.

Pute skimmed the coil of paper. "October 1943 joined Metropolitan Police Training School as cadet. October 1946 admitted to basic training . . ."

Quimper knew that too. "I, Adrian Russell Quimper do solemnly and sincerely declare and affirm that I will well and truly serve our Sovereign Lord the King in the office of Constable . . ."

Quimper had joined the police because he had been brought up to be of use. He was too young for the war and had toyed with medicine and the law before realising that, unlike his brother Hugh, he lacked the academic flair for either. But he had the capacity to endure, and patience. He delighted in physical fitness and physical courage. He had a logical kind of mind that was attracted by the careful piecing together of facts and the process of deduction. Above all he believed in an intrinsic order of things. It was these qualities that made Adrian Quimper admirably suited for police work.

Right from the start he'd wanted to work in the CID, to be one of those people indistinguishable from the rest, who observed and calculated, and finally pounced. Looking back on it now, Quimper realised, that he had always been attracted by the clandestine exercise of power.

"January 1947, attached to D Division — Paddington police station."

No one was accepted into the CID straight away. Whoever you were you had to start at the bottom, pound the beat as a constable, continue the learning process begun at training school. Fortunately, at the time Paddington was one of the busiest stations in the metropolis. Due perhaps to its proximity to the railway terminal it was surrounded by slums and the streets of the manor were filled with prostitutes. Quimper had enough opportunities for the exercise of his many talents.

"1949 — Completion of probationary training. Appointed temporary Detective Constable." That had been the first important step in Quimper's career. Temporary detective constables, then as now, were called aids. Then as now you were expected to average over one hundred arrests in a two-year period. Quimper remembered that time well. He had worked sixty hours a week and his total score had been one hundred and seventy-two arrests.

"February 1952 — Appointed Detective Sergeant, second class."

By the time he became Detective Sergeant, Quimper knew

that arrests alone were not enough. It was convictions that counted and not only because they helped promotion. The most exasperating experience any policeman could suffer was to watch helplessly while a man he *knew* to be guilty walked smiling out of the dock.

By February 1952 Quimper was experienced in nudging evidence along. A twist here, a shift of emphasis there, and he took pride that not even the shrewdest mouthpiece could talk his client out of a sentence.

It was not the kind of thing that the ordinary man in the street would have understood or condoned. But it was necessary. Otherwise the law would be a laughing stock, and the manor filled with villains. In any case, Quimper did not need understanding. He accepted that no one understood, except another policeman or a villain. At the time Quimper was content, doing his job as best as he knew how.

"November 1953 — Recommended for special course leading to promotion as Detective Inspector."

The villains he was dealing with were bigger and tougher and more experienced. Now he even came across policemen who would help *them* along. And sometimes it needed more than just a casual twist to the verbals, or a shift of emphasis in the rendering of evidence to secure a conviction. Sometimes Quimper felt he had to do things that made him as big a villain as the man he was prosecuting.

Nevertheless he was content. He was recognised as one who was doing well in his chosen career, someone who through diligence and persistence was destined to ultimately reach the top.

"December 19th, 1953 — Adrian Russell Quimper was suspended from police duty while the Department of Public Prosecutions considered whether he should be charged with manslaughter."

Quimper remembered the 19th December 1953 very well.

It was six days before Christmas. The West End was decorated with fairy lights and a mist hung over the city like smoke after a bombing raid. The pavements were crusted with frozen slush, the streets ridged with snow that had turned brown from the continuous passage of tyres.

Quimper left the station at twenty past one that morning. Because he was a careful man, because of the state of the roads and because it was the season of parties and drunks, he drove slowly towards his flat in Kilburn. He was still driving slowly when he turned the Austin A30 on to one of the snow-covered side streets filtering off Kilburn High Road. It was a short-cut he usually took, and as he left the bright lights behind, he turned his headlamps on against the mist.

The road was deserted. It was cold and damp. London was a city that went to bed early. Nothing moved in the street except for the figures crouching in the doorway of the tobacconist, forty yards away. At first Quimper thought they were men buying cigarettes from a machine. Then his lights picked out the glint of glass lying on the packed snow. Quimper doused his lights and pulled into the kerb, stopping a few yards before the shop.

He opened the door of the car and got out, moving too quickly, slipping momentarily in the snow. At the same moment the two figures charged out of the doorway. One came straight at Quimper, shoulder charging him as he tried to keep his balance, spreadeagling him on the snow.

Quimper grabbed at the man's ankle, but the man was travelling too quickly. His foot tore out of Quimper's grasp like a stone flying through water. Quimper swore and twisted himself up, slipping in the snow, falling, damp seeping through his clothes.

By the time he was on his feet the man was a fading shadow, melting into the mist and the haze of the lights at the end of the street. Angrily Quimper climbed into his car. The other man had run in the opposite direction, away from the brightly lit streets.

Quimper turned his headlights on full beam and drove into the mist. A few yards further on he saw the second man, a furtive figure walking quickly along the edge of the pavement, huddling close to the buildings.

As the car lamps blazed heavily through the mist, the figure began to run. Quimper accelerated, feeling the car switch-back gently on the soft-packed snow. Quimper accelerated until he was five yards behind the running figure and shouted: "Stop!"

The figure continued to run, bending low, feet making chunking noises in the soft snow. Quimper moved the car after him, drawing steadily closer. Suddenly the man stopped and turned.

A hand went under the bulky sweater and emerged, bearing the ugly black shadow of a gun. Quimper saw the man brace himself, hold the gun out at arm's length and Quimper accelerated.

He twisted sideways behind the wheel and thumped the car over the pavement, feeling it buck and twist like a runaway pony. The man turned, tried to sidestep, slipped. His mouth opened in a scream of terror, then the stubby bonnet of the A30 got him with a soft cracking sound, like snow falling off a roof.

By the time Quimper got out of the car, the man crushed between the radiator grille and the wall was dead.

His name was Nicole Pavese and he had been big for his age. The eighteenth of December had been his sixteenth birthday.

They had found four packets of Players in his trouser pocket and the gun he had pointed at Quimper had been a present from an uncle who had a fruit stall in Naples and who had been visiting his sister's family in London, for the first time in fourteen years. At Milan Airport the visiting uncle had bought his nephew a birthday present of a toy Luger. It wasn't any good, not even for shooting at pigeons.

"January 1954 — Adrian Russell Quimper resigned from the Metropolitan Police."

Quimper remembered that too. He remembered the lean, cat-like man with the pale translucent eyes who had called himself David Carruthers and who had told Quimper he understood. He knew the guilt, and the frustration, and he appreciated initiative and ambition. At the time Carruthers had seemed like his only friend, and most important Carruthers had offered Quimper a way out.

In February 1954 Quimper joined R Section of the Department. In his new role he was not concerned with the problems of evidence, and a few months after he joined the Department he was posted to Cyprus.

"What did you do in Cyprus?" Pute asked. "The printout doesn't say."

"Nothing," Quimper replied, "nothing very much."

He couldn't tell Pute that his job in Cyprus had been more than that of a policeman. Even more than that of an investigator. Sometimes, Adrian Quimper had been judge, jury and executioner.

22

IF ONE HAD SUFFICIENT FAITH, it was surprising how easy it was to kill another human being. And at the beginning Quimper had faith. At the beginning Quimper was content.

He was content to savour the primitive excitement of the chase, to share in the intellectual delight of planning each operation to its minutest detail in the full knowledge that the slightest mistake could turn him in one ghastly moment from the hunter into the hunted. Quimper was stimulated by the danger of his new occupation, and the proximity to death, as always, brought a heightened awareness of life.

It was this awareness that made him accept the long, patient waiting, the hours and days when nothing happened and he had to force concentration. He accepted the rigidity of schedules and the need to calculate angles and distances and velocities. At the beginning Quimper learned to live with a gun, to direct his life towards that single climactic heart stopping moment when his finger squeezed the trigger.

But only at the beginning.

After all, as Carruthers had pointed out so clearly, if Quimper had been two years older he would have participated in the great push across France and into Germany. And would he not have killed then? And killed more indiscriminately?

The fundamental ethic had not changed since 1945. There was still a war on. Only the enemy was different. That and the rules.

One no longer killed with stacks of thousand pounders, pulverising sleeping cities into debris and ashes. One no longer used tanks and infantry and artillery. In this new and secret war the targets like the guns were hand-picked. One used hand guns fitted with silencers so effective that the explosions were like muffled coughs, rifles with telescopic sights, capable of picking a man out at one thousand yards.

And in time one got used to the idea of killing. Almost used.

Quimper could recall the precise moment when he had begun to lose faith. It was late on a summer's evening, in a hotel in Istanbul.

From where he stood he could hear the continual bleat of traffic jamming the wide swathe of river they called the Golden Horn. The man he had come to see was a sad-eyed Rumanian with a torso like a miniature Mr. Michelin. Because the Rumanian had been waiting impatiently for his contact and was hoping that he wouldn't have to miss his plane and stay yet one more night away from home, he opened the door at Quimper's knock.

Quimper shot him three times with the silenced Smith and Wesson Airweight.

The impact of the bullets flung the man across the room, against the bed and the opened suitcase. Petals of blood blossomed against the striped collarless shirt, pumping out of the curved little tummy between the braces. The man hit the bed and slumped slowly down on to the patterned Turkoman carpet. He thrust a hand out helplessly, his face freezing with horror. And all the time his body was sliding to the floor he

117

kept staring at Quimper with dark uncomprehending eyes that were hurt and unbelieving and innocent.

It was so easy after that. For the first time since Quimper had begun to work for R Section, he thought about what he was doing and why. And in time, thought made him impotent.

For the first time Quimper realised that he was in a world that was neither black nor white but predominantly grey. He realised that governments, even his own, were rarely omniscient and even more rarely virtuous. Most of all, he realised that, as at Nuremberg, acting under orders was no excuse.

Inevitably there were other jobs after Istanbul. And just as inevitably Quimper performed them with scrupulous accuracy. But the doubt within him festered, and by the time they sent him to Beirut, the doubt had become a certainty.

*   *   *

"They want to talk to you," Vivian was saying. "They say they've finished."

"What? Who?"

"The fingerprint men, silly. Who else?"

Quimper ran a hand across his face, pulling his moustache against the side of his lips. It had been a mistake to ask Pute to show him his file. It disturbed too many ghosts.

"And Carruthers called. He wants to see you right away."

Quimper stared at Vivian, blankly.

"Oh Quimper! For heaven's sake! Wake up!"

"I was thinking," Quimper said. "Thinking. We've got quite a problem here. With Amory dead and all that."

Vivian clicked her tongue with annoyance. "Well, whom are you going to see first? The fingerprint men or Carruthers?"

"Carruthers can wait," Quimper answered.

The fingerprint men came into the room. Quimper spoke

to the shorter man, the one with the case. "Anyone stop you coming out of Records?"

"No," the man said.

"They're supposed to," Quimper said.

The fingerprint men had made two positive identifications. Pute and Kumar. There were a few others but they were too faint to be of any use.

"Fine," Quimper said. "Thanks." That was just about what he expected.

* * *

Carruthers's office was on the first floor, a few doors down from McGregor's. It was smaller and exquisitely furnished in Regency style. Carruthers had a private income and Quimper hoped that the rope-back Trafalgar chair and the Carlton House writing table had not eaten up too much of Carruthers's capital. The room was bare of all papers, filing cabinets, and other appurtenances of an office. With its furniture and Chinese rugs it looked more like the reception room of a knocking-shop in the Regent's Park than that of the assistant head of the Department.

Seated on the edge of a second rope-back chair, as if he were afraid his weight would break it, was Harvey Milner.

Carruthers said: "I spoke to Pute five minutes ago. The tapes are still missing."

"Yes," Quimper said with what he hoped was reassurance. "I'm looking into it."

"Good heavens, man! We need more than that. We need answers, fast." Then the voice lowered itself to a whisper. "What are you doing?"

Quimper hesitated. Somehow Carruthers always made him defensive. There was very little he could do about it, though. Once you had worked for Carruthers you were permanently

119

on the defensive. "I've asked Pute to search the entire basement and even turn out the men's lockers. I've had the safe checked out for fingerprints. There's nothing there."

"What else?"

"There's an absentee. Someone called Cooper and one of the operators has left on holiday. I've alerted the ports to do a stop and search. And after lunch I want to talk to Pute's assistant."

"Adrian, all this takes too long. You aren't doing police work any more. We've got to have results within hours."

"And the best way of getting results is by following standard police techniques. Let's eliminate the innocent, then we can deal with the guilty."

Carruthers said: "Those tapes may be half-way to Russia by now."

Quimper remarked mildly, "We don't even know if they have left the building."

Carruthers stared into space, six inches above Quimper's head. Quimper began to feel even more uneasy. There was something altogether too remote, too impersonal about that stare. Finally Carruthers flicked his hand towards the other man in the room. "You've met Harvey Milner."

Milner shifted gingerly in his chair.

Quimper studied the lean face with the hollow cheeks and the crew-cut fair hair. Milner was wearing an open-necked knitted shirt under a dark sports jacket. The jacket was sufficiently well tailored to hide the holster under his arm. He wore freshly pressed dark blue trousers and rubber-heeled moccasins that looked as if they were handmade. There was no doubt that Harvey Milner looked after himself. But then most professionals did.

"Hello, Harvey," Quimper said softly.

"Harvey will be working with you," Carruthers said.

"Now look, David — that's impossible. I have my own job to do —"

"And you've no time to play nursemaid. Well you'll find there's no need for that. Harvey has had three years with the Los Angeles police."

"Doing what?"

Milner said, "I was a detective, second class."

"Fine," Quimper said and turned to Carruthers. "I don't need a trained policeman helping me. I don't need anyone. This is a simple, routine investigation. That's all."

"There's a lot at stake, Adrian."

Quimper went silent. He was aware of that. He was aware that this was possibly his last chance to prove that he was more than a has been drifting towards an early retirement and government pension.

"Adrian," Carruthers asked, "have you thought what will happen when you find the person who took the tapes?"

Quimper hadn't thought of that.

"You might not even get a chance to caution him. Isn't that what you policemen do?"

"I'm not a policeman," Quimper snapped angrily. "And I'm sure that I can handle anything that turns up."

"Anything?" Carruthers asked. "Are you sure? Are you really sure?"

Their eyes met and locked. Both men were aware that they were thinking of the same place and the same time. They were both thinking of Beirut, of a hot and sunny hill and a worried, tired face framed in the cross hairs of a gunsight.

"Harvey comes with you," Carruthers said, softly, "and Harvey stays with you. And that's an order. For your own safety as much as anything."

Quimper looked away, unable to face this final humiliation.

121

Of course he didn't have to work with Harvey. He didn't have to look for their stupid tapes. He could always resign.

Resign, the word brought back memories. He remembered the soft, stuttering, voice persuading him, advising him, telling him that no job, no country was worth the loss of his integrity. That if he felt the way he did, he must resign.

But that had been many years ago. And Quimper knew he had much less courage now than he'd had then, that retirement was still a luxury he could not afford.

23

Harvey Milner stood in the car park and looked at Quimper's Rover 2000. Quimper had bought the car second-hand four years ago. It was painted a dull grey, and the camouflage aspect was increased by a liberal sprinkling of bird droppings, dead leaves, and streaks of livid brown rust. The car appeared to sag on its springs, a hub cap was missing and the bumpers were pressed into the bodywork and had long ago given up any pretence of gleaming.

"This yours?" Milner asked.

Quimper nodded. He had no love for cars or the cult that surrounded their acquisition and performance and shape. To Quimper cars were means of transport, nothing more. They were more comfortable than trains and sometimes more efficient. The only time he'd thought about this car was when it broke down, which the Rover 2000 rarely did.

"It's all yours?" Milner repeated.

"Yes," Quimper replied, "why?"

Milner suppressed a smile. "We'll go in mine," he said.

*   *   *

Alex Cooper, the technician who had not turned up for work that day, lived in Dollis Hill. They went in Milner's

Porsche, a low, yellow monster that seemed to scud along the ground at an alarming speed.

Quimper lay back in the contoured leather seat and marvelled at the amount of leg room he had. "This is really a Security Section matter, you know," he said.

Milner didn't take his eyes off the road. "Amory was R Section," he said.

"Did you know him well?"

"No."

"So there's nothing personal, then?"

Milner flashed him a sideways glance. "Nothing's ever personal."

Milner drove with an effective mixture of deftness and aggression. They went up the Edgware Road in spasmodic bursts of acceleration, past shop windows crowded with amplifiers and headphones and hi-fi tuners, went round gigantic earthworks of a new flyover towards Kilburn and Neasden where the small factories began.

Quimper asked: "How long have you been with the Department?"

"Long enough."

Milner was lying back in his seat, arms stretched straight out to the steering wheel. His jacket had come undone and the butt of the Colt protruded in front of his chest.

"Got a licence for that thing?" Quimper asked.

"Of course."

"Always preferred a waist clip, myself."

"Did you?"

"Yes. Used a Smith and Wesson Airweight .38 Special."

"Very swish," Milner said.

"I always preferred revolvers," Quimper said. "Automatics jam."

"Only if you're nervous," Milner replied.

They came down the farther side of Shoot Up Hill, bordered by car showrooms, last year's gleaming models crowding the pavements, windscreens obscured by price tags.

Quimper remembered when he too had been confident. When he too had the sense of power that comes with the ability to kill. Power over life is the supreme power. You take away a man's life and you take away everything. He knew what that had been like.

They came past Dollis Hill underground station and turned down the rows of semi-detacheds stretching all the way to Gladstone Park. Houses with bay windows and coloured doors, with little paved paths and porches with pointed roofs, small gardens ablaze with foxgloves and geraniums.

Quimper thought he would have liked to live in Dollis Hill. It was neat, orderly, suburban. But then Quimper had no need for a house. His few possessions did not even fill the one-room flat he rented in Bayswater. A house was no good if you lived alone.

It would have been different, he thought, if Amaryk were still alive, if he'd had the courage to marry her. Quimper forced himself to stop thinking. Sit back and enjoy the drive, he told himself, enjoy the mildewed sunshine pouring through the visorless windscreen. Listen to the burble of the exhaust and think about Amory and Alex Cooper and missing tapes that were big as cans of film but don't think about anything else. Especially about Amaryk.

"Sixty-eight isn't it?" Milner was already slowing the car down.

"Yes."

They stopped by a waist-high iron gate with a path leading to the mauve door.

"Right," Milner said. "Let's go."

Quimper rang the bell. After a long silence there was the

thumping of someone coming down the stairs. A rattle of locks, the door opened a fraction, held by a length of chain. Even in Dollis Hill there was fear.

"Who is it?" A voice croaked.

Quimper glimpsed a rheumy face, a frail pyjamaed dressing-gowned body, heard a sniffle and gazed into watery eyes.

"Mr. Cooper?"

"Yes." Irritation and self-pity made the word sound like a challenge.

Quimper hesitated. "We are Jehovah's Witnesses," he said. "We wonder if you would be interested."

"No," the man said, "go away! I am ill. Can't you see I am ill."

The door slammed. The length of chain rattled. Milner and Quimper walked between the low hedges of evergreens to the car.

"Looks like he needs salvation," Milner said.

"Don't we all," Quimper replied. "Don't we all."

                    *   *   *

V. V. Kumar, Assistant Programme Controller, lived in a flat in Belsize Park. A visiting card by the bell push announced the fact that he had a Master of Science Degree and you had to ring the bell three times. At the third ring the door opened and a little old lady came out. "Good morning," she cried, "lovely day."

"Morning," Quimper replied, with equal heartiness.

The sky was the colour of lead.

The old lady trundled a wicker shopping basket down the rain-damped steps. Obligingly, she had left the door open.

They went up dark stairs with worn carpets, passed locked doors and empty landings to the third floor. The wallpaper, stained and scarred with the passage of numerous tenants, had faded a long time ago. Light filtered through grimy windows.

Milner knocked on the yellow door with the lopsided figure three.

The door opened. A large-eyed Indian face peered through the crack.

Quimper said : "Mr. Kumar?"

The eyes fixed on Quimper, the expression on the round dark face became less wary. "Mr. Quimper isn't it? From Security?"

"We'd like a word with you," Quimper pressed against the door. "If you have the time."

Kumar stood back and allowed them to enter the flat. He was a round-shouldered, plump man, short, wearing an open white shirt that dangled over a vividly striped sarong. His feet were thrust into fleece-lined carpet slippers.

"It's about the Kiriov tapes," Quimper said, walking through the small lobby into the lounge. The lounge was surprisingly large. The floor was covered with rush matting and there were two thick sofas at right angles to each other in front of the fireplace. In the middle of the room was a low table on which stood a chess board and replica pieces of early Norse chessmen. Joss sticks smouldered in front of a small Hindu icon on the wall and the place smelt of incense and flowers and spices mixed with oil.

"I was just going to sleep," Kumar said. "I've been on night duty."

"We won't be long," Quimper said soothingly. "It's important about the Kiriov tapes. They're missing."

Kumar said : "That isn't my fault, Mr. Quimper. For the answer to that you must direct your questions to others."

"But you worked on the tapes?"

"I work on many things. All figures, all the time. If I

127

worked on this programme why should I remember it more than any other? I am only an assistant. I do what I am told."

"Are you saying you know nothing about the Kiriov tapes?"

Kumar hesitated. The thick liver-coloured lips moved and were restrained by a pinch of white teeth. "That is what I am saying, Mr. Quimper. The Kiriov tapes were not my responsibility."

For the first time Milner spoke. "You have any theories about how the tapes got out of the building?"

"No," Kumar said.

"Do you know anyone in Records who might be a Communist?"

"We're too busy to discuss politics."

"Anyone who might be a pacifist? Or a liberal of any kind? Anyone who might be against the war in Vietnam?"

"No," Kumar said. "We have no time to talk of such things."

"Know any SDS-ers, anyone who belongs to or is associated with the Weathermen or the Youth International Party or like underground groups?"

Kumar shook his head. "No."

"Know any perverts, homosexuals, members of Gay Lib? Know anyone who takes drugs?"

"For goodness' sake!"

Milner stepped right up to Kumar. "Alright Charley, what's that smell?" he demanded.

Kumar sniffed. "It's — it's the joss sticks."

"I know they're joss sticks, Charley. Why are you burning them?"

"Because I always —"

"Because you've been smoking dope, Charley, we know you've been smoking dope." Suddenly Milner grabbed Kumar by the shirtfront. "Right Charley, tell us about your pothead friends who took the tapes. Tell us why you helped them do it." Savagely he thrust his face right up against the dark rolling eyes of the Indian. "Talk, Charley, before I bust your teeth."

Quimper moved. An arm grabbed Milner by the thick fuzz of his crew-cut and yanked his head back. Then with vicious deliberation he slammed the heel of his other hand against the bridge of Harvey Milner's nose.

Milner reeled back, eyes tearing, releasing Kumar so that he fell across the chessboard. Quimper saw Milner's hands flail, reaching underneath his coat.

"Don't," he snapped, moving in close, preparing to grab the man about the body.

The phone rang. Kumar clutching his sarong with one hand picked up the receiver. "For you," he said to Quimper.

Slowly Quimper turned. The ringing of the phone bell had somehow acted like a release. Milner pulled out a handkerchief and dabbed at his tearing eyes. Quimper noted with satisfaction that the handkerchief came away spotted with red.

He took the phone from Kumar and said: "Quimper."

Quimper listened briefly. Then he said: "Thanks. One of us will go along."

He put the phone down and said, "Immigration in Dover think they've got Hetherset. He has a boot full of film cans with him."

Milner still dabbing at his nose said: "That's it, then."

"Not quite. The man says he isn't Hetherset. He claims to be a film director going abroad for the COI."

Milner put away his handkerchief and straightened his jacket.

"One of us will have to go down to Dover and talk to him."

"Why?"

"If he is from COI, then there will be hell to pay."

The two men stared at each other.

"You'd better go," Milner said at last. "He'll need someone with a kind heart."

Quimper said simply, "You're the one with the car."

*　　*　　*

After Milner left, Quimper knelt down and began to re-arrange the chess pieces. "Don't worry," Kumar said. "it was only a chess problem from the paper. I can soon get the moves right."

Still kneeling, Quimper asked: "Whom should I talk to about the Kiriov tapes?"

Kumar asked: "The tapes that were in the safe?"

Quimper nodded.

"You should talk to Pute. After all, he's in charge."

Quimper stood up and dusted the knees of his trousers. "I wouldn't know what to ask Pute. I'm not a technician, you see."

"Ask him about the night shift. Ask him about his wife. Ask him about his movements, Mr. Quimper, the night before last."

Quimper asked: "How do you get on with Mr. Pute?"

"Personally," Kumar said, "I like him."

Quimper waited, looking straight into the angry, dark face. "But there is something wrong?"

Kumar turned away. "I know what you are trying to do, Mr. Quimper. You are trying to protect Mr. Pute." Abruptly he turned. "Please go. I want to sleep."

24

QUIMPER GOT A TAXI back to the office, noting down the 80*p* fare and the 15*p* tip in his book. Vivian had left a note for him.

England are collapsing. I have gone to Lords. You can get in after the tea interval for 50p.
P.S. I am owed seven days' casual leave.

Quimper crumpled the note and phoned down for Pute. Questioning Pute up here would make matters more formal. It would also make Pute more uncomfortable.

Pute came in looking more nervous than ever.

"Sit down," Quimper said. There was no mister now, no recognition of their being colleagues. After Pute had sat down Quimper got up and very deliberately shut the door. It was symbolic. It often had the effect of making a suspect feel trapped.

Pute said: "I hear they've found Hetherset. Carruthers phoned me for a description."

Quimper stifled his irritation. The whole problem with an investigation this size was that everyone treated it as their responsibility.

Quimper said, "Tell me about the keys to the safe. Were they always under your control?"

"Mine, or Mr. Kumar's."

"You're sure of that? You never had any occasion to let anyone else open the safe? For any reason?"

"No."

"You're sure."

"Yes."

"And the keys were always in your possession, or Mr. Kumar's? Is that right?"

Pute nodded.

"What happened if either of you weren't there?"

Pute said, "Let me explain. We work three eight-hour shifts. Kumar and I rotate them between us. During the one shift that isn't covered, the holder of the key remains on call."

"What precisely does that mean?"

"The person on call remains at home. If he goes out, he reports his movements to Records and leaves a telephone number where he can be contacted."

"When," Quimper asked, "did you last do a night shift?"

"The night before last. I was on two till ten."

"I mean ten to six in the morning?"

Pute clasped his long hands between his bony knees. He reminded Quimper of a pony he had once seen, smelling fire for the first time. There was the same mixture of incredulity and panic.

Pute said: "I see Mr. Kumar has been talking about his grievances." He smiled thinly.

Quimper didn't say anything. Hostile silence was also effective in making a suspect talk.

"Kumar wants my job," Pute admitted. "He feels I am too old for it, too far removed from recent developments. He wants to install a new computer, on the lines of the IBM

System /3, with random access discs. With disc storage we would be able to get at information much faster." Pute stopped and looked across the desk at Quimper. Quimper gazed impassively back.

"There's another thing, too," Pute said. "It's nothing to do with me." He leaned his body forward. "Kumar feels he is being discriminated against. Because he is foreign."

"And is he discriminated against?"

"Most certainly not. I personally have always recommended him most highly in my annual reports." Pute paused. "You can verify that."

Quimper said : "Tell me about your wife."

Pute's face broke. "My God," he cried, "My God! How Kumar must detest me! And for what, Mr. Quimper? I have never harmed him in any way."

"Tell me about your wife," Quimper repeated.

Pute sat upright, the change in posture somehow giving him dignity. "My wife is nothing to do with the Kiriov tapes," Pute said. "She is a sick woman, Mr. Quimper. She suffers from a heart complaint and it is necessary that someone stays with her all the time. During the day I have a trained nurse. We have no children, you see."

Quimper nodded sympathetically.

"It is the nights that are difficult. It is difficult to get someone to stay with her all night."

"So you pass the ten at night to six in the morning shift on to Kumar?"

Pute nodded. "It was within my rights."

Quimper asked : "Should you not have told someone here about your problem? We might have been able to help."

"I thought about that, and discussed it with my wife. But I am fifty-four, Mr. Quimper. The retirement age gets lower all the time and you read so much in the papers these days

133

about the respectable unemployed. I was frightened, Mr. Quimper. Computers, after all, are a young man's job and Kumar is right. I am getting too old for it." He paused. "All I — we wanted, was three more years."

Quimper asked gently : "What happened the night before last ?"

"Kumar was late. His car had broken down. He phoned and asked me to cover him for half an hour. At ten thirty I phoned Kumar and told him I couldn't afford to wait. I live in Harrow and even late at night it takes me a good forty-five minutes to get back."

"And ?"

"Kumar said he would be leaving soon. His battery had been stolen and the Blue Star people were outside fitting a replacement. He wouldn't be long, he said, about ten minutes or so."

"So you left ?"

"It was only a matter of ten or twenty minutes. No more. How could I have known that someone would have stolen the Kiriov tapes in that time. It's never happened before."

"What did you do with the key ?" Quimper asked.

"I left it in the top drawer of my desk. As usual."

He looked miserably down at his hands, still trapped between his thighs. "I am sorry, Mr. Quimper. I should have been more candid with you."

Quimper ran a weary hand along his face. "Why is there no back-up information on the tapes? Punch cards, programmes, that kind of thing. I understand that normally this back-up information is stored for some weeks. Is that so? And isn't the back-up information normally stored separately ?"

"Normally," Pute said. "Yes."

"What happened this time ?"

"Everything that was not immediately relevant was destroyed. The rest was stored with the tapes."

"Why?"

"Those were C's orders. Everything was very secret."

Quimper picked up a pen and began to revolve it slowly round in his hand. "Do you have a copy of C's orders?"

"No," Pute said, "they were verbal."

"Verbal? You mean telephoned?"

"No," Pute said. "I mean verbal. C came to my office."

"C came to Records?"

"Amory reported to C verbally. Then Amory reported to me, also verbally. C wished to check that our reports tallied."

"And did they?"

"Except for one small matter. Amory forgot to tell me that a Leftist Youth Movement was involved. They called themselves the Red Gnomes."

"Sounds like a football team," Quimper murmured.

But Pute did not appreciate the joke.

25

"HETHERSET," THE CUSTOMS OFFICER said, "Hetherton. You must admit the names are similar." But Alan Hetherton was not to be soothed. He had been held up in Dover nearly five hours. He'd had his luggage searched, his film exposed, and worst of all seen Melinda dragged away, protesting volubly to be searched by two lady customs officers. Melinda hadn't spoken to him since.

"You haven't heard the end of this," he promised. "There'll be an inquiry. And a fuss in parliament."

The customs officers groaned silently. Alan Hetherton was working for the Central Office of Information. Alan Hetherton had been on his way to Brussels to film the Prime Minister meeting the Chancellor of Germany and the President of France. And now some keen officer had checked his cans of film through an X-ray machine. The customs officer was certain that it would not end here.

"We are trying to arrange an RAF Heron," he said, "to fly you to Brussels."

"Damn it, man, it's too bloody late. The Prime Minister must be sailing back in his yacht by now."

The customs officer sighed. He hoped that at least the BBC had been able to get a film of the occasion.

*　　*　　*

C's staff were well used to gentlemen who wanted to meet C urgently and would not state their business. Quimper was kept waiting only a few minutes before being led down labyrinthine corridors to the great man's room.

It was a splendid room, overlooking the park with an original painting by Sir Winston Churchill. There was a large conference table surrounded by twelve chairs and a whole array of leather chairs arranged around the fireplace. There was plenty of carpeted space framed with pictures of former prime ministers and groups of cabinet ministers looking like superannuated cricket elevens. The ceilings were high and everything had a rich gleam to it.

C did all of his work at a small desk in a separate ante-room. He reserved this magnificent chamber for visitors. When Quimper entered he was standing with his back to the dead fire, hands clasped behind him.

"Adrian Quimper," he cried. "I thought you'd retired."

"I did," Quimper replied and added, "sir."

Quimper perched on the edge of a sofa and C took one of the armchairs. There was a silver tray and cups of Minton china. There were, unfortunately, no sandwiches.

C poured out the tea. "Old soldier, eh? You too. Never die, Quimper, eh, what?"

"No, sir," Quimper replied, thinking that the only opportunity you got to fade away was if the KGB didn't get you first.

Steely-blue eyes fixed themselves on Quimper. "What did you want to see me about?"

"The Kiriov tapes."

"Ah! You've found them."

"No, sir. Not yet."

"But you will Quimper, eh."

Quimper sipped his tea, Twining's Earl Grey. "I'm actually checking out a story, sir."

"Ah," C breathed. "Good."

"Mr. Pute, head of Records, tells me you instructed him to destroy all back-up information on the Kiriov tapes."

"That's right, Quimper. Quite right. Can't afford to let them fall into the wrong hands, you know."

"And you also instructed him to keep all the information in the one place?"

"Quite correct."

"We can't replace the information, sir," he said.

"That's why you will have to find the tapes, eh, Quimper?" C sipped his tea and replaced the cup with a tiny clink.

Quimper frowned. What he had to say was going to sound ridiculous. "I was just checking that it was in fact you who gave these instructions, sir. You see — I thought — perhaps someone masquerading —"

C shook his head. "I did, Quimper. We had to have absolute secrecy."

"And it was you who told Pute about the Red Gnomes?"

"Yes. Just as well too. Amory had forgotten about them. But they're not important, Quimper. A crowd of ragamuffins — hippies — live like gypsies. Travel behind the Curtain. Used as couriers, no doubt."

Quimper asked, "Sir, do you remember what Amory told you?"

"There were names, mostly. Addresses. I've already sent McGregor a list of what I do remember." C stood up. "Do you think Pute will get us another tape?"

"I hope so, sir," Quimper replied, standing up also.

C walked Quimper to the door. "You will keep me informed won't you, Quimper?"

"Yes, sir."

"Good, good."

At the door C caught Quimper's arm above the elbow. "Quimper."

"Sir?"

"You resigned, didn't you? Illness or some damn thing, no doubt."

"You could call it that." Quimper said.

C smiled. "Never mind, Quimper," he said. "It's nice having you back again."

*　　*　　*

On the way back to the office Quimper saw that England had lost eight wickets for one hundred and thirty-two runs. Vivian's presence at Lords had apparently been of as little benefit to England as it normally was to the Department. Grinning sourly, Quimper went along to his office. The door was open. Carruthers was seated behind his desk.

"David, what —"

Carruthers leaned back in Quimper's chair and fixed him with the translucent eyes.

"I'm taking you off the Kiriov case," he said softly.

"You can't," Quimper said. "I'm just getting somewhere with it."

"Was it you who ordered a port alert for Hetherset?"

"Yes."

"Well they got someone called Hetherton."

"But that's hardly my fault."

"Hetherton works for the COI. He was on his way to film the Prime Minister in Brussels. Not only was he prevented from doing that but some idiot exposed his film. We've had the COI on to us, the Prime Minister's office, the Home Office, someone called Bridgenorth and one gentleman from the *Daily Telegraph*."

139

"But —"

"The only people who haven't called us are the CIA. And they'll be round as soon as they've read the newspapers."

"You've got to listen —"

"I was always opposed to your handling this case. Now we've got a public display of incompetence."

"It isn't —"

"And that's not all. C's been on wanting to know if you are all right. Apparently you spent the afternoon with him, babbling about verifying his instructions."

"I was checking Pute's story. It's usual procedure."

"Damn procedure. Where the hell are the tapes?"

"I'm trying to find them, aren't I?"

Carruthers stood up. "Not any more," he said softly. "My section will take over now. I will want your report in the morning."

26

QUIMPER STAYED LONGER than usual in the Nag's Head that night, talking to Charlie the barman and Ned who had been at Ypres and Mr. Soames who owned the local florists. That night Quimper ate at the Nag's Head and talked about the weather and the quality of beer in the new metal casks and the road widening scheme the Council was trying to push through. And all the time he kept telling himself that the Kiriov tapes weren't important, that he had retired from active intelligence work many years ago, that it was work best left to younger men and to bastards like Harvey Milner.

He remembered that he hadn't vetted Harvey Milner. It was his job to vet everyone joining the Department except the computer people who were independent of him. Milner wasn't a computer person. Therefore Quimper should have vetted him. He promised himself that he would inquire into it the next morning, and that, he thought, would upset Carruthers.

He went home carrying the Dewar's in a brown paper bag. Pute had made him remember, brought back memories tipped with poignancy and pain. That night Quimper went back to his orderly one-roomed flat and listened to Dvorak, and drank Dewar's and thought about Cyprus.

* * *

He had been in Cyprus fourteen months, two weeks and one day, working out of that strange establishment housed in the forest near Athalassa, that was known locally as the stud farm. It wasn't even a farm.

Officially it came under the British Middle East Office, but Quimper doubted whether even they knew what really went on amidst the underground installations and the radio masts.

In those days Quimper had not been used to the job and he had often gone to Kyrenia to get drunk. In any case there was nothing much else to do on the island and Quimper had found an excellent drinking companion in the craggily handsome ex-diplomat, who like Quimper had left England under a cloud. It was this shared sense of rejection and injustice that first brought them together. That and the coincidence of their first names being the same. They had both been christened Adrian Russell.

It was in Kyrenia that he met Amaryk. She was one of those westernised Cypriot girls who wore skirts and rode a Vespa scooter. She worked in a hotel, and sometimes she would have a drink with Quimper, and occasionally go swimming with him.

The day Quimper was ordered to kill the Armenian, all that changed.

The Armenians are a widespread community. They are to be found in Britain, in the United States, in France, throughout the Middle East and the Levant. They have always been persecuted and always oppressed. They have always had excellent means of communication. The community in Cyprus was no exception. They could send messages anywhere and for an Armenian the Iron Curtain simply did not exist.

This particular Armenian was in frequent contact with fellow countrymen in Soviet Armenia. What concerned the Department was that the traffic was only one way.

As usual, Quimper had planned the job meticulously. It was a hot day and he had a long drive ahead of him. Quimper had an hour to spare and he wandered into the hotel in Kyrenia, to talk to Amaryk and have a beer.

That visit probably saved his life.

The other Adrian Russell had been there with Amaryk and they had been about to go looking for Quimper. In view of what happened ten years afterwards, Quimper wondered whether his friend had been altruistic then, or merely protecting his own lines of communication. But that day, in the hotel in Kyrenia, Quimper had been grateful.

His friend said the Armenians knew what he was going to do. He told Quimper when and where and how he was going to do it, and that the Armenians were waiting for him, with men who had been specially brought to the island to get rid of Quimper.

Amaryk had taken him away from Kyrenia. They had gone to a little village where they had stayed for ten days. When they came back, they had rented a small white house near the beach, with pomegranates in the garden and the sound of waves pounding on the sand. And they had been very happy.

The time in between jobs became the best time. Amaryk stopped working and they spent whole days spread out like pinned insects against the scorching Mediterranean sun. They rented cars and drove to Limassol and Nicosia, they went skin diving, and in the evenings, more often than not, they used to go to the cinema, to see one of those cowboy epics that Amaryk loved.

And always, in those days, they made love.

When Amaryk became pregnant, Quimper decided she must have the child. Abortions in Cyprus were tricky to arrange and to execute. Besides he knew Amaryk wanted the

143

child. He was very much in love with her and asked the Department for permission to marry her.

At first the Department procrastinated. Then they reasoned. It wasn't fair to her, they said. Had he thought what would happen if he was posted away from Cyprus? Did he not know that men in his vocation had a short life expectancy? Couldn't he see that it wasn't right for anyone, most of all for her?

Two months after he had applied for permission to marry Amaryk, Quimper was posted back to England.

Of course, he could have fought it. Of course he could have resigned. That was what his friend, the ex-diplomat, told him he should do. Resign.

But the Department was more powerful than that, and they said he would only be away for a few months. They promised him that he would get a foreign posting again. They promised him . . .

He was not in Cyprus when his daughter was born. Six weeks after the child's birth, the *sherut* taxi Amaryk was riding in drove over a mine. All eight occupants were killed instantly. Amaryk couldn't have suffered any pain.

*   *   *

Quimper went over to his desk and took out the letter and turned the record over.

Amaryk's family had brought up the child. Occasionally he had thought of having her with him in England, but that was impossible.

In the beginning he had gone to Cyprus every year, but as the child grew older he had realised the embarrassment he could cause and stayed away. After that he had only sent them money.

He unfolded the letter and looked at the spiky, unformed handwriting. "*Dear Father,*" They had told her after all. She had been nineteen when she had written. She had wanted to leave Cyprus. She had met an American boy and wanted to marry him. She was writing to ask Quimper's blessing, and for money.

Quimper had sent her far more than she had asked and he had met her between flights at Heathrow.

She was as old as Amaryk had been when he first met her, and there was Amaryk in the bright dark eyes and the wide, generous mouth. She was shorter than her mother had been, and more plump. Their meeting had been uncomfortable, as stilted and formal as her letters.

She still wrote to him dutifully, informing him of the birth of his first grandson and of the second. In her last letter she had invited him to visit America and stay with them.

It was something he should do, Quimper thought. She was still his child, and he owed Amaryk something.

PART III

"The first duty of an underground worker is to perfect not only his cover story but also his cover personality."

Kim Philby,
My silent War

27

QUIMPER CAME IN LATE the next morning, thick-headed, stale-mouthed, feeling as if he should have his head amputated.

"Morning," he said softly. Noise was painful.

Vivian stared at her shrouded typewriter and said, "It's terrible."

"Yes," Quimper said. "One hundred and fifty-six all out. On a good wicket too."

Vivian sniffled. "It isn't that. It's Pute."

"What's the matter with Pute?"

"He's dead!"

Vivian sniffled again.

"Dead! How?"

"He fell out of a window."

"But that's impossible! He works in the basement."

"He fell out of the window of McGregor's office."

*   *   *

Out of deference to the dead and the draught in McGregor's office, they held the meeting in Carruthers's room. McGregor was there, ashen under the normally healthy countenance, and Carruthers, looking more subdued than usual. The only person who looked normal was Harvey Milner. It was Harvey

149

Milner who had seen Pute plunge through the window of McGregor's office.

"I had the seat of my car fully reclined," Milner said, "below the level of the body work. I waited for him in the car park."

From the room next door came a faint sound of hammering. It reminded Quimper of the time he had been caught in a Turkish village, trapped in a vicious crossfire between British troops and EOKA guerrillas. And all the while the shooting had been going on, the village carpenter had been hammering out coffins.

"He came, lemme see, at quarter to three, ten to three, something like that. He had a large briefcase with him and he was walking very fast. I let him try opening his car before I got out. 'What you got in that case?' I asked. He was so scared he dropped the car keys. He looked as guilty as hell. 'Actually,' he said in that fancy voice of his, 'I'm on my way home.' I told him I was from R Section and wanted to look in his case. He said I didn't have any right."

Milner shrugged. "We struggled a little and I got the case open. It was filled with spools of tape. 'You taking work home or something?' I asked. He said: 'Leave me alone. I have my orders.' "

Milner shrugged again. "I took him upstairs and had someone from Records check the tapes. They were duplicates of some of the tapes already in Records. And you know something else? Pute hadn't logged that he was making any spare tapes."

"I said to Pute, 'That's it then. We've got you fair and square. We know you're on a ten o'clock flight to Vienna. So you may as well come clean and tell me everything.' "

"He began to babble about harassment, and wanted to talk to David and to C and to the Queen and God knows who else. I told him he wasn't going to talk to nobody and that he was going to stay right there in the office until he told me everything." Milner paused and looked carefully at the other men in the room. "I roughed him up a little bit, to show that I was serious."

Quimper asked softly. "And did you drop him out of the window to see if he would bounce?"

Milner said, "He wasn't making sense. He was babbling a lot about how someone had to protect the tapes and that there was a spy in the Department and that he had a Grade 1 clearance." Milner shook his head. "He just wouldn't believe we had him cold. Just wouldn't believe it. Musta been shock or something. Anyway I gave him a shot of rye from my hip flask. Kind of soothe him down a bit, you know. But it didn't do any good. He went on babbling, denying everything more than ever."

Milner stopped and looked at the back of his hands. "I told him he wasn't doing himself any good. That if he co-operated we'd go easy on him. He musta been mad or something. He just laughed. He was sitting at the opposite side of the desk to me. Suddenly he stopped. Got up. Came across to me. He had a fixed smile on his face, like he was in a trance."

"I thought he was going to take a punch at me. So I stood up. But he went right on past me. And jumped."

Milner stopped and shifted uncomfortably in the silence that followed his statement. "Jesus!" he said, "I didn't know he was going to do it. He musta been crazy."

"Pute wasn't a spy," Quimper said.

"What makes you so sure, Adrian?" McGregor asked.

Quimper shook his head. "I talked to Pute most of yesterday. There were lots of things he was and a lot more things he wasn't. But he wasn't a spy. After a while you get to sense these things."

"Did you know," Curruthers asked, "that Pute fought with the International Brigade during the Spanish Civil War?"

Quimper did not know that. What he did know was that Spain in 1936 had been something special. Not everyone who had joined the International Brigade had done so because they were Communists.

"That doesn't prove anything," Quimper said.

"But it shows a trend," Carruthers replied. "A trend. A direction."

Quimper tried to visualise Pute as a gangling stripling of twenty, hefting a carbine, drilling with an ill-assorted squad of troops. No, that picture didn't fit. Then he remembered the quiet pride in Pute's voice when he had told Quimper of his religious convictions. Then everything fitted. Almost.

"How did you know to wait for Pute?" Quimper asked.

Milner shrugged. "Got a tip off."

"Who from?"

"Who d'you think? His chick."

Quimper frowned.

"It's always the chicks," Milner said. "They always let a guy down."

"You mean his wife told you?"

"I mean his chick. His girlfriend. She's a stripper in, where do you call it — Greek Street."

Quimper let out a soft, low whistle. "You mean to say that Pute was shopped by a stripper?"

"Yhep."

"Tell me more," Quimper said softly.

Her name was Indira Devi. She was an Indian dancer who performed an act called "The Unveiled Kama Sutra" at a

152

club called Le Chic Chick. In the past few months Pute had, according to Milner, been balling her regularly.

On the night the Kiriov tapes had disappeared, Pute had picked her up after her last performance. They had driven to Hampstead Heath. There Pute had handed over what looked like a spool of recording tape to someone in a parked car.

The girl had thought nothing of it at the time. She was used, she said, to men doing unaccountable things.

The evening before his death, Pute had telephoned her from a call box. He was in trouble, he said. Someone called Quimper had been asking him too many questions and he had to leave the country. He wanted her to accompany him.

Pute said he had powerful friends abroad who would help them with a job and money. It would be very nice, he said. They would have a house of their own and she wouldn't have to work. He wanted her to get two tickets on the BEA flight to Vienna at ten fifteen the next morning.

"How did you get in touch with the girl?" Quimper asked Milner.

It was Carruthers who replied. "She got in touch with us," he said. "She didn't want to leave England. She likes it here."

"I don't believe it," Quimper said.

"Suit yourself. But remember, *we* got the results."

Milner was reaching into his jacket pocket. He took out two brightly coloured air tickets and dropped them on the desk. "You better believe that," he said shortly.

Quimper looked at the tickets, framed with the winged symbol of BEA. They were in the names of Mr. H. Pute and Miss I. Devi. They were for flight number BE 700 which had left Heathrow hardly two hours previously.

28

THERE WAS NOTHING MORE to do after that, except write his report. Quimper went back to his office and began dictating. His head still ached with a pain as cloyingly persistent as condensation sticking to cold glass. He drank two cups of Blue Mountain coffee and took two aspirins. They made hardly any difference. The way he felt had very little to do with his headache and the amount he had drunk the previous night.

Vivian straightened her skirt and rested her notepad on the desk. "Hardly fair is it, Quimper, taking you off the case like that?"

Quimper said, "It doesn't matter now. It's all over."

Vivian lit a cigarette. A thin mist of blue smoke hovered between them. "Do you think Pute was a spy?"

"No," Quimper said and thought that spies were the most unlikely sort of people. The ability a spy needed most was the capacity to live a double life. For years people had believed that Abel was only an artist and Eleysa Bazna, merely a valet. Couldn't Pute have been something more than a civil servant who operated computers? Could the year in Spain have been a glimpse of a lifetime of secret dedication?

"I don't believe Pute was a spy, either," Vivian said.

But everything fitted together, Quimper thought. It was as

neat as one of the integrated circuits in Pute's computer. It was too neat. If Pute had been set up, Milner wouldn't have overlooked a detail like the air tickets. Anyone could buy an air ticket and he didn't have to use his own name to do so.

"Quimper," Vivian asked, "what are we going to do about it?"

"Do about it?" Quimper hesitated. "Nothing," he said. "The file is closed."

"But if Pute wasn't a spy, then there is a spy running loose in the Department."

Quimper shrugged. "That's Carruthers's problem. Don't you worry about that. Carruthers will find him."

"And throw him out of a window?"

"Pute jumped," Quimper said tightly. "Of his own accord and free will, Pute jumped."

Vivian said, "If you believe that, you'll believe anything."

"The file is closed, Vivian. Damn it, don't you realise what that means. It's finished. Over." Quimper made a chopping gesture with his hand.

"And what does that mean to you, Quimper? Another door shut? Something else you cannot face up to?"

"Oh for God's sake, shut up! I've got nothing more to do with it."

Vivian looked him directly in the face. "You have everything to do with it, Quimper. You can't let them do this to Pute. You can't let them do this to you."

Quimper looked away from Vivian. They had been doing it to him for nearly twenty-five years. He should be used to it by now. What was it the man said? The appetite grows on what it feeds upon.

Vivian ground out her cigarette. "Quimper," she asked matter of factly, "what the hell has happened to your balls?"

*   *   *

155

All his life Quimper had a need of belonging. At first there had been the school, and afterwards the police, even R Section of the Department. More than most other men Quimper needed the security that came from working for something vaster than himself. His particular brand of selflessness needed the purpose and direction and effectiveness that came from being a member of a team. That was why when R Section had no further use for him, he had rejoined the police.

He had come back to the police more experienced, more mature, in a strange way more capable of dealing with the obtuse logistics of power. Promotion had come quickly, almost without effort on his part. At forty he had held the rank of detective inspector. That was when he had gone after Luigi Scallo.

It would have been easier to have watched, and taken note, and done nothing. Much easier to pretend that the things Luigi Scallo did were only the result of a diseased society, that he wasn't doing too much harm, and that his friends did not exist. But Quimper hadn't been like that. He hadn't had enough sense to step around the fallen body, he had not known how to walk with unseeing eyes.

In the end Quimper had got Luigi Scallo. In that at least he had succeeded, even though it was a messy business.

He hadn't realised how many friends Scallo had bought and how many he could now condemn by implication. Quimper was told he had been imprudent, that, he should have waited. Now they were all in danger and the best thing would be if Scallo did not give evidence on his own behalf. The best thing would be if they did a deal with Scallo, had him plead guilty in exchange for a lighter sentence.

But it was wrong, Quimper had protested. Everyone agreed with him, but there was a practical problem and it required a practical solution. There was enough public unease about planted evidence, about rhinoceros-hide whips and fiddled expense accounts. Besides, there wasn't sufficient proof and there was also the question of Quimper's own relationship with Scallo. It would suit everyone concerned if Scallo were dealt with quietly and Quimper were to resign. The guilty could be punished afterwards.

Of course Quimper had received his full gratuity, and of course his file showed the resignation as voluntary. But Quimper had been unemployed for eighteen months after that.

Those eighteen months had, he thought, finally given him cunning. For eighteen months he had written three letters of application every week. For eighteen months he had received about two replies a month. And most of the time there had been something wrong. He was too old, he was too young, he lacked the experience that was required, they couldn't have an ex-detective inspector counting the petty cash. On the few occasions that things had seemed right, there was a question of references, of discreet telephone conversations and inevitably someone would mention Luigi Scallo.

During that time Quimper had spent some of his gratuity on setting up his own detective agency. He had taken a shabby office at £1,500 a year above a Greek restaurant in Charlotte Street and had bought furniture and a typewriter and engaged a secretary.

It was no good. With a new business you needed capital and you needed contacts, lawyers who would give you divorce work, financial directors who would require you to guard their payrolls and protect their building sites. After three months Quimper surrendered his lease and gave his secretary four months' wages. He didn't get much for the furniture or the typewriter.

He felt rejected, useless. The only alternative was working as a gunman, but he preferred starvation to that.

McGregor's offer of a job had been a relief. More than that. Salvation. He was back on a government payroll and his years of service would count towards his final pension. Ten years ago the last thing he'd thought about was a pension. But as one grew older, Quimper reflected, one's choices became more limited and security became increasingly important. Now all he had to do was keep his head down and do his job. What he should do was leave the question of spies in the Department to Carruthers. He needed to be disinvolved.

Quimper thought briefly about Pute and Amory and Milner and Carruthers. He thought about the significance of the Kiriov tapes. There was enough of the policeman left in him to want to know more. Besides his whole upbringing precluded dis-involvement. All his life he had been taught to be of use. Somewhere there was a victim and somehow Quimper felt responsible.

He thought it over very carefully. No one in the Department kept a check on what he did or where he went. No one, he thought, need ever know. It wouldn't do any harm just to inquire, to probe the surface.

When he went out into Vivian's office, he told himself that was all he was committed to do.

Vivian looked up from her typing. "My God! You look ill!"

Deliberately Quimper poured himself a third cup of Blue Mountain. "Do you think you could get a copy of the autopsy report on Pute?"

"Yes. Surely."

"And do you know Kumar, down in Records?"

"God's gift to the science of mathematics."

"You know him that well?"

"Yes. He also knows some terrific curry restaurants."

"You mean you've had dinner with him?"

"Why not?"

"Nothing," Quimper said. "Could you get me a printout on Milner?"

"Yes." Vivian said.

"I'm going out," Quimper said, "I'll be back later this afternoon."

"Should I tell anyone where you'll be?"

"Yes," Quimper replied. "Tell them I've gone to a strip club."

*   *   *

But first Quimper went to Harrow, where the evergreen borders were nearly as high as a man, and even the azaleas were ordered. Here amid the self-sufficience and the privacy, he met Mrs. Pute.

She was a small, chesty woman, her whole attitude governed by diminutiveness. She wore gold rimmed spectacles, and an old black dress. She had not been prepared for mourning.

"I'm from the Department," Quimper said clasping the dry hand, brittle as bird's bones. "I knew your — I knew Pute."

"You worked with Henry?"

Quimper started. To this woman, he had been Henry. To Amaryk, Quimper had been Ariano. It was difficult to imagine.

"Yes," Quimper said. "That's right."

"It's good of you to come."

Quimper looked round at the cosy drawing room, the china souvenirs on the mantelpiece and the pale Pisarro prints. He looked at the flecked wallpaper and the flying geese arrayed on the wall. This, he thought, had been home. This was home. Loneliness had not yet made its mark.

"I liked Pute," Quimper said.

"Everyone did. He was on the Council you know. And the Computer Society sent a wreath."

She showed him.

Quimper shuffled his feet. "There are some questions," he said. "I have to ask some questions."

She looked at him expressionlessly. "No," she said. "No. Go away. Get out. Don't bring your muck in here. You people have already done enough to him."

29

GREEK STREET FESTERED under summer rain, neon lights bubbling wanly. Head waiters in short white jackets and bow ties stood in doorways, looking both bored and expectant. A crowd of men, tieless, their coats shabby and much creased milled around the entrance to a betting shop. Traffic moved hesitantly between lines of parked cars.

The street was not yet awake. It was an old street that had seen everything, so it woke late, crustily, it came alive sour-faced and liverish, knowing there was nothing new, especially the rain.

Le Chic Chick was situated half-way down the street.

Quimper hurried past the cinema posters and the empty building plastered over with tattered advertisements, past door-ways with broken bell pushes where stained, biroed cards announced: *"Sandra — French lessons — Walk right up."*

Le Chic Chick had once been a shop. Now, nearly lifesize photographs of nearly naked women filled the plate-glass window which had once displayed packets of Gold Flake and tins of Old Holborn. Quimper glimpsed breasts like air ships, thighs like plaster columns. He stared at the hard, inviting faces and the rigid artificial smiles. A girl cowered at the feet of a male apache dancer, a girl thrust tits and bound wrists at the wet street. The brazenness revolted Quimper as did the sheer acreage of bare flesh.

Indira Devi was the only girl who appeared in the window, fully clothed. A garish notice announced:

SEXY! SEXY! LIKE YOU'VE NEVER SEEN BEFORE!
MYSTERIOUS EASTERN TECHNIQUES!
AN EXPERIENCE OF A LIFETIME!

The girl herself looked demure. She stood in the rigid posture of the Indian classical dance, legs splayed apart, body twisted to one side, head bowed in line with outstretched tips of fingers. She wore what Quimper supposed would be an Indian costume, thin, loose-fitting trousers fastened above the ankle, a small ornamented bodice, a pointed tiara, arms full of bangles. The expression in the large, dark, sloe-like eyes, was remote. She had a good figure, good skin, delicate breasts. Somehow, in that shop window, surrounded by all those shamefully contorted bodies, she looked vulnerable.

Quimper became aware of a man standing too close to him. A slim young fellow wearing a shiny leather jacket and flared pink trousers. Quimper glimpsed a lean, tanned face, a pair of cuban-heeled boots made from artificially aged leather. Despite the rain, the man was wearing large sunglasses that swept round his temples, like goggles.

The man gave Quimper a conspiratorial smile. "We'll be open in ten minutes," the man said. "Then you can see it all — in the flesh."

Quimper felt embarrassed that he should be taken for one of the regular raincoat brigade. Did he look as old as that? Or as lascivious?

"The girl," he said pointing.

"Wonderful," the man said. "Never seen anything like it

162

in all the time I've been in Soho. She'll be on at twelve thirty."

"I was wondering," Quimper said, "about her National Insurance cards."

The man looked puzzled.

"I'm from the Ministry of National Insurance," Quimper said. "Just checking. You own this place?"

"Yes," the man admitted. "Sort of."

"Fine," Quimper smiled. "Shall we go in then?"

They went in and down a narrow wooden stairway, across a room with a row of chairs, a bar at one end, a small stage at the other. A man in a flowered shirt fiddled with a large spotlight with a circular disc like an artist's palette in front of it. Quimper followed the man with the shiny leather jacket behind the stage, up another flight of stairs into a small office crammed with paper and old calendars. A crusted mug stood on one windowsill. A locked door led to another part of the building and beyond the grimy window, Soho glistened drably.

The man opened a drawer, took out a petty cash box and five National Insurance cards.

Quimper glanced cursorily at them. "Five employees?"

"Barman, lightman, soundman, cleaner, and one girl."

"What about you, Mr. er —"

"Maasten," the man said. "Nicholas Maasten. I'm not resident."

"Not resident?"

"No," Maasten said.

For the first time Quimper realised that Maasten still had his sunglasses on. "I suppose that's all right then," Quimper said.

"I suppose so."

"What about the girl?" Quimper asked, "The Indian girl. Doesn't she have a card?"

"She's casual," Maasten said.

"But she must have a card. I suppose I'd better talk to her."

Maasten gave him a thin smile. "I suppose you'd better," he said and walked to the door. At the door he turned. "I'll send her in to you the minute she comes in." He gestured towards one of the filing cabinets. "There's some Scotch in one of the drawers. Help yourself. I just want to check the lighting."

Quimper waited. He even helped himself to a glass of Scotch.

*　　*　　*

The girl came in, her clothes damp from rain. She wore a white belted mackintosh, low-heeled casuals. A mauve scarf covered thick glistening hair. The expression on her face was wary.

She was even smaller than Quimper imagined, and she looked even more vulnerable.

Quimper cleared his throat. "I'm from the Ministry of National Insurance," he said. "I've come about your cards."

Maasten had followed the girl into the room. He was standing by the door, leaning against the jamb. He had taken off the sunglasses. His eyes were a deep, unwinking blue. Quimper turned to him. "I wonder," he said, "it's got to be private. Regulations, you know."

Maasten shrugged shiny leather shoulders. "Oh sure," he said, "help yourself."

The girl turned quickly as Maasten left the room. Then she turned back to Quimper. The wariness was replaced by a genuine nervousness. "I have not got a National Insurance card," she told him, speaking rapidly. "I do not know how to get one. Perhaps you will tell me."

Quimper said, "Tell me about Henry Pute."

She started, the colour draining from her face. The large eyes grew even wider and she stuttered, looking for words. Finally she asked, "Who are you?"

"I'm a kind of policeman," Quimper said, "Now tell me about Pute."

She placed her hand upon her white plastic handbag. "I don't — don't know."

"Henry Pute," Quimper said. "You saw him handing tapes over on Hampstead Heath. He was your boyfriend, remember? You used to sleep with him. Tell me what you know about him. Tell me about the times he used to meet you at this club? Tell me how he offered to take you to Vienna?"

"Go away," the girl muttered, "go away."

The door crashed open. Maasten stood there. Standing behind him were two burly men, with closely shaved heads, thick flattened noses and the slow scarred eyes of punchies.

"Mister," Maasten said slowly, "you got a card or something to show where you are from?"

Casually Quimper reached into his pocket and took out his wallet. He flicked it open, looked into it, put it away, looked up at Maasten and said, "I'm frightfully sorry. I seem to have left it behind."

"Yes," Maasten said. "It could happen to anybody."

Quimper said: "Awfully stupid of me."

"What's your name?" Maasten asked abruptly.

Quimper hesitated. "Adrian Quimper," he said.

Maasten held out his hand. "Give me the wallet," he said.

Quimper looked quickly around him. The only way out of the room was through the door. Either that, or a running jump through the window into Greek Street. He handed over

165

the wallet. He knew what happened when you jumped out of windows.

Maasten flipped through the wallet, stopping at the cancelled warrant card. "Ex-cop," he said quietly. "What's it now? Private work?"

"Yes," Quimper said.

Maasten looked at the driving licence, the Barclaycard. He flicked through Quimper's cheque book and came to his Ministry of Defence identification card. Maasten stopped. He let out a soft whistle and said: "Like bloody hell you're private."

Maasten sent the bouncers away and shut the door after them. "Lesson one," he said looking directly at Quimper, "get your facts straight. The Ministry of National Insurance has for over six years been calling itself the Department of Social Security. Secondly, you pay stamps for all the time you're working in this country — resident or not."

He handed Quimper back his wallet. "Next time, you might be needing a spare face," he said. He sat down and lit a black Sobranie. "What gives with the girl?"

"It's about Pute," the girl cried. She hesitated. "He was asking me about a man called Pute."

Maasten waved his hand. "That's enough, love." He turned to Quimper. "What about Pute? You were checking his National Insurance cards as well?"

"Did you know Pute?"

"I never had the pleasure."

"He's dead."

"Really! Tragic circumstances, was it?"

"He fell out of a window."

"Hard," Maasten said, "on the reflexes."

Quimper stood up. The Scotch had done wonders for his headache. "I'd like another," he said.

166

"Go ahead."

Quimper poured out a drink. "There were a few things wrong with Pute's death," he said. "For a start, it all fitted together too neatly. Also, the man they tell me Pute was, wasn't the Pute I knew."

"Who wants to find out about Pute?" Maasten asked.

"I do. I think Pute was framed."

Maasten laughed. "As an ex-copper, you should know."

"I do know, and that's why I'm trying to find out why."

Maasten let out another of those soft whistles. "A straight copper!"

"I'm not a copper, damn it. I liked Pute."

Maasten said, "A butch copper," but the humour had gone from his voice.

Quimper finished his drink, while Maasten finished his black Sobranie. Quimper thought that this whole interview wasn't going the way he'd planned it. For a start, this man, Maasten had far too much self-confidence. Most people who lived on the fringes of the law, lost all confidence at the first intimation of authority. By their very nature they feared the law. By their very nature, they were guilty. Maasten was different. His self-confidence had more to it than mere cockiness. There was more to Maasten than the shiny leather jacket and the flared trousers. Quimper remembered that he had recognised the Ministry of Defence identification card.

"Know a man called Carruthers?" he asked.

"Know lots of people," Maasten replied.

"David Carruthers," Quimper said, "head of R Section."

"No one's named Carruthers," Maasten said. "Not even in a book."

"This one is," Quimper said. "And he's real."

"Carruthers isn't his real name," Maasten said, thinking that the head of R Section was up to his old tricks again.

Maasten thought that he'd love to do Carruthers right in the translucent eyeballs.

Quimper put his wallet away. "Pute wasn't involved," he said. "He was only a computer technician. He was only doing his job. I wonder how he was set up."

Maasten lit another cigarette. He took a couple of drags and said, "I'd try immigration. They're the same kind of bastards as policemen." He got up and walked to the door. "Or National Insurance Inspectors."

Quimper thought Maasten was smiling. Quimper thought he liked Maasten.

*   *   *

After that it was easy. Indira Devi was from East Africa. She could stay in England for only three more months. She wanted to stay in England for the rest of her life. East Africa was no place for Asians.

Besides she had a boyfriend, back home. She wanted him to come to England too and she was working to earn enough money for his passage.

"I did not sleep with Henry Pute," she said, "I only said I did, because Nicholas said it would be all right. That if I helped these people they would help me."

Quimper said, "I suppose they promised they would let you stay in England."

She nodded quickly. "They also said they would let my boyfriend in."

"Do you know who asked you to do this?"

She shook her head. All she knew was that Nicholas had told her it would be all right, and that Nicholas was a good man. All she remembered about the man who asked her to lie about Henry Pute was that he wore a pin-striped suit.

168

30

"OH THERE YOU ARE," Vivian cried through a mouthful of lettuce and cheese and Hovis. Her typist's chair was tilted back and she was balancing herself precariously by the pressure of her feet against the desk. Quimper glimpsed her large rounded knee and muscled nylon thigh, thought uneasily of the pictures of the window of Le Chic Chick and poured himself a cup of Blue Mountain.

"What happened?" he asked.

"The autopsy report isn't done yet," she said.

"Oh," said Quimper.

"But I've got a rundown on it from one of the assistants. Pute was killed by the fall." She took a large bite out of the sandwich. "He'd been full of booze. Scotch they think."

"It was rye."

"Rye?"

"American Scotch. What did you find out about Milner?"

"Nothing."

"That's impossible. There must be a card down in Records. Everyone's got to have one."

"Milner hasn't," Vivian said.

Quimper went into his office, frowning. Vivian followed, carrying a large plastic box. "There's smoked salmon on rye or cheese on Hovis," she said.

Quimper blanched at rye. It made him think of Pute's

dissected body, spread out on a marble slab. He took the cheese on Hovis.

"He used to be with the CIA," Vivian said.

"Who?"

"Milner of course, silly. Who else?"

"How do you know?"

"I asked Heathcote of R Section. He worked with Milner six months ago, in Paris. The Service de Documentation Exterieure have got a file on him."

"And we haven't?"

"If we have, it's classified Grade O," Vivian said. "No one's seen it. According to the French, Milner worked for the CIA in Vietnam. He was part of the Phoenix Programme — the one that eliminated suspect Vietnamese."

"I thought the Phoenix Programme was Vietcong propaganda."

"You're naïve, Quimper. The French are right. They still have good contacts in Vietnam and they know the Phoenix Programme existed."

"And Milner?"

"He got too violent, even for them. It seems he killed a village headman and his entire family, and the CIA had to make him non-operational. Since then he's been scratching a living in Paris, working when he can as a freelance gunman."

Quimper stopped chewing. Of all the various kinds of killers there were, freelances were the worst. Their only motive for killing was money. They had no loyalty and they had no emotions. The only good thing about them was that they were highly professional. He picked up the phone and put it down. "What the hell is a freelance doing in R Section?" he asked. "Especially one with a record like Milner's?"

"That's what we're going to find out, aren't we, Quimper?"

Quimper groaned. "If Milner doesn't find us first."

Vivian laughed. "Now you. Tell me what you found out."

Quimper told her. When he finished, she asked: "Maasten must know who told the girl to lie about Pute. Didn't you see Maasten afterwards?"

"No," Quimper said. "He'd left the club. Besides I think he's told us everything he was going to say."

"Shame," Vivian said. "I'd like to have seen him. He sounds quite dreamy."

Quimper went silent, thinking. He wasn't feeling at all dreamy. Finally he said, "Mrs. Hetherset, she'd know."

"She'd know what?"

"One of the technicians who was working the night the tapes disappeared is on holiday. No one knows where he has gone. I knew his family. Perhaps Alistair Hetherset told his mother where he was going on holiday."

"Good!" Vivian cried, "that's really positive thinking."

"There's one thing, though," Quimper said, "I don't know where Mrs. Hetherset lives."

"What's the last address you have?"

Quimper gave it to her. Vivian studied it and said, "Won't take long. Leave it to me." She picked up the plastic box and started to walk from the room.

"Vivian," Quimper said, "how do you get all this information?"

She turned and smiled at him. "You forget, Quimper, I've worked in every section of this Department." She waved the piece of paper with Mrs. Hetherset's address. "For this, I think I'll try Pensions. Young Hetherset isn't married. He must have named a next of kin." She opened the door. Her smile became broader, "Did anyone ever tell you Quimper, a boy's best friend is his mother."

Which wasn't exactly true in the case of Alistair Hetherset.

171

31

Mrs. Hetherset lived in Colney Heath, a pleasant Hertfordshire village, surrounded by farm land, trapped between the wide arterial swathes of the A1 and the A6.

Quimper drove out feeling exhilarated. The morning's rain had ceased and a silvery sun had appeared. He could smell grass and earth through the open car window. Recklessly he took the Rover 2000 up to its maximum. At ninety the steering began to feel light and Quimper began to feel quite debonair. For no reason that he could explain Quimper also began to feel excitedly free.

He swooped off the A1 on to the A6, wheeled around a roundabout on a narrow road, sped past fields and thick woods. The edges of the road were muddy, the grass squashed grey and flat by the continual passage of farm vehicles.

Mrs. Hetherset lived in a small house at the end of a gravel drive. Behind the house, electric pylons marched across the fields towards the north-east.

Mrs. Hetherset was a capable-looking woman in her early sixties. She still had a good figure and her movements had a briskness that belied her age. She was wearing sensible tweeds and even more sensible-looking brogues. Her hair was blue-rinsed and behind the pink hornrimmed glasses, her eyes were bright and sharp.

"Adrian Quimper," she said to him. "Good God! I remember you as a boy. Good cricketer too. At least Alistair thought so. Captained the team didn't you?"

"No," Quimper said, "that was my brother, Hugh."

"I'm sure it was you Alistair thought was the better cricketer. I can't think why."

Quimper remembered. It had been one of his rare moments of glory. Playing against a neighbouring school Quimper had opened batting and had been 164 not out at the end. The local paper had had his picture in it and described his innings as controlled and professional.

"Alistair used to think you'd play for England one day," Mrs. Hetherset said.

Quimper laughed. "I wasn't really even county standard," he said.

"Now that you're here, you must stay to tea."

"I wouldn't dream of imposing —"

"Not at all dear boy. I'm simply dying for someone to talk to."

Over nut loaf and herbal tea they spoke of the school and Quimper's parents. They spoke about people whom they had, in their different ways, both known, and whom Quimper saw occasionally at Hugh's. By the time he had to refuse a second cup of herbal tea, Quimper gently turned the conversation to Alistair.

She spoke about Alistair, eagerly at first, relating stories of his childhood and adolescence. At one time Alistair had wanted to be a painter, but she'd soon put a stop to that. He now worked for the government, he was, she said, in computers.

"I know," Quimper said. "I work there."

"Are you in computers too, Adrian?"

She made it sound like being in the Royal Enclosure at Ascot.

"No, no," Quimper said. "I work for the government too."

Mrs. Hetherset frowned. "You were in the police weren't you?"

Quimper smiled. "Still am."

The frown behind the slanted pink hornrims became more pronounced. "Oh dear, you haven't come about the accident. I didn't think — I mean — isn't there some kind of professional etiquette about arresting people one knows?"

"No," Quimper said. "And I didn't come about the accident."

"I'm so glad. I know everyone says it, but it wasn't my fault."

Quimper asked, "Could you tell me where Alistair is?"

Mrs. Hetherset looked at her wristwatch, a gold banded Omega. "At work."

"He's on holiday, Mrs. Hetherset. I was wondering if you knew where he'd gone."

"He isn't in trouble, is he?"

"No," Quimper said. "It's just that a problem has come up at work, and we'd like to contact him."

The face behind the pink hornrims went very set. The slack skin beneath the jaw was taken up. "I don't see much of Alistair any more," Mrs. Hetherset said. She looked out of the window, freezing her gaze midway along the fields. "Not since he met the girl."

"I see."

"You haven't met Jane, have you?"

"No," Quimper said.

Mrs. Hetherset said, "I didn't think so. She's not your

type at all." She looked back into the room. "She's a very modern young lady, which means she's selfish and headstrong and unkempt. I don't believe she had been very well brought up." Mrs. Hetherset paused. "I can't stand her."

"Maybe," Quimper ventured, "with time . . ."

"I can't stand the way she's taken Alistair over," Mrs. Hetherset said fiercely. "She's turned him round completely. He even had the gall to accuse me of ruining his life. If it wasn't for me he wouldn't now have a roof over his head or money in his pocket. Coming between a mother and her child. That is the sort of woman Jane Brewster is."

Mrs. Hetherset's outburst subsided. In a softer voice she said, "You know, Adrian, I don't see Alistair these days. I'm not even sure that I want to."

*   *   *

Quimper left soon afterwards, driving fast back to London. The afternoon had grown quite scorching. Pollen and scraps of fluffy white dandelion floated in the air. The grass smelt dry and dusty.

Quimper was thinking that it was a gorgeous day, and funny how Mrs. Hetherset had remembered him, and shame, he would have to search Alistair's flat. He was thinking that he would have to do it properly and that he would have to ask Detective Superintendent Bridgenorth to get him a search warrant. Quimper was thinking that it was a lovely afternoon on which to play cricket, to laze in the outfield, feeling the sun warm on one's back, and listen to the thwack of willow meeting leather. Seeing the roundabout rushing up at him, Quimper braked harshly.

The grey bonnet of the Rover 2000 erupted, momentarily suspended on a ball of orange flame. The windscreen slivered,

175

blew out. Wind and flames whipped at Quimper's face as the car swerved across the road and slammed diagonally into the kerb. Tyres burst. The suspension collapsed. Quimper was flung forward and upwards against his seat belt. With locked, flattened wheels, the car dry-skidded across the kerb leaving great black scars and a trail of dragging metal. It gouged through the ribbon of grass verge, shot clear across the ditch below it, smashed through a clapboard fence.

Partly held by his lap and diagonal, Quimper thumped against the door and the roof. Wrenching, thudding, clattering noises filled his ears. Flames roared in front of him.

The car smashed through the clapboard fence, hit the field on one wheel and rolled end over end.

Sky and earth and flames disintegrated and mingled. The gear lever stuck into Quimper's ribs, the steering folded like molten plastic. He was flung against seat and roof lining, he was surrounded by a rattling and a clattering and a roaring.

Suddenly it all ceased. He lay on his side, across the seats, and there was silence. Except for the crackling of the flames and the searing heat.

Slowly Quimper unfastened his seat belt. Then, more quickly, he crawled along the passenger's seat and through the window into the field.

The car lay on its side, burning furiously. Metal twisted like a living thing and the paint streamed off in a grey river. Quimper forced himself to run. He had to get away before the flames reached the petrol tank.

His body ached all over, and there was a specially sharp pain above his ribs. A speckled curtain danced before his eyes and the inside of his lungs felt pressed together, arid. His feet moved over the stubbled grass like those in a film shot in slow motion. He glimpsed a row of parked cars on the road above him, a line of interested faces.

With a whooshing sound like a train rushing through a tunnel, the car exploded. Quimper felt himself sucked up by a huge vacuum then thrown face down on to the earth. The grass smelt dry and dusty, Quimper lay on his face and tried to force himself to stop trembling.

32

SUPERINTENDENT BRIDGENORTH GLARED at the little boy with carefully disguised distaste. The boy had just launched a Ford GT40 at Bridgenorth's boot.

"You wanna see my computacar," the boy asked. "It drives all by isself. Mam, where's my computacar?"

"Later," the boy's mother said. "The gentleman wants to ask you some questions."

"That's right, Johnny," Superintendent Bridgenorth said. "I want to ask you some questions."

"His name's Timothy," the boy's mother said.

"Timothy," Superintendent Bridgenorth said, "I want to ask you some questions."

"I want my computacar," Timothy cried and bounced the GT40 over Bridgenorth's boot.

Bridgenorth gave the boy a pained smile. "Timothy," he asked, "how would you like to make sixpence?"

Timothy whipped the GT40 away and looked searchingly at Bridgenorth. "You mean $2\frac{1}{2}p$?" he asked.

"It isn't right," Timothy's mother said, "to offer children money."

"I was only trying to be friendly," Bridgenorth said. His smile was beginning to hurt.

"I want my computacar. Mister, will you give me another computacar?"

"If you promise it to him you have to give it," the mother warned.

"I will," Bridgenorth said, wondering how the devil he would explain *that* in his expenses.

"Timothy," the boy's mother said, "there, the nice gentleman will give you a computacar if you will answer his questions."

Timothy glared balefully at Bridgenorth. "What do you want?" he asked.

"Tell me, Timothy," Bridgenorth said, "about the car you saw the other night."

"We won't get into any trouble," the boy's mother asked. "I mean giving evidence and all that, my husband would be furious —"

"No," Bridgenorth said. "There won't be any trouble. Now, Timothy, tell me about that car."

"What do you want to know for?" Timothy asked. "It was a cruddy car. It wasn't fast like the GT40 or the Ferrari. Wanna see my Ferrari?"

"Mr. Bridgenorth doesn't want to see your Ferrari, darling," the boy's mother said. "He wants to ask you some questions about the car you saw the other night."

"Why?" Timothy demanded.

"Because," his mother explained, "Mr. Bridgenorth is a policeman and the car was used by some bad people in a robbery."

"It was a Humber Imperial," Timothy said. "Black, with one of those funny aerial things on the roof."

"How are you so sure?" Bridgenorth asked.

"Because I looked, silly."

"Now, Timothy that's no way to —"

"Are you sure it wasn't a Humber Hawk?"

"It had Imperial written all over it."

"Are you sure, Timothy?"

"Yersss. I looked."

"What made you look?"

"Because there aren't many Humbers. They stopped making them any more. They're cruddy cars. Not like the GT40."

"I see," Bridgenorth said and stood up. "Thank you." He had no doubt that this boy was telling the truth. And if that was so, Bridgenorth realised that he was in far deeper than he ever wanted to be.

"Was it helpful?" the boy's mother asked.

"Very," Bridgenorth said and started to leave the room.

From the floor Timothy launched the GT40 at him. It skidded along the carpet, took off on a ridge and hit Bridgenorth painfully on the shin.

33

THE DOCTOR SAID that apart from the singeing and the bruises, the loss of two teeth and the badly swollen cheekbone, Quimper was definitely suffering from shock and quite probably from concussion. Doctors, like policemen, were experts at separating the definite from the probable.

The doctor would not advise — here he paused and looked searchingly at Quimper — that Quimper discharge himself. Most definitely he would not advise that.

Quimper was unable to look searchingly back at the doctor. The bruised cheek had puffed and discoloured, the swelling had nearly closed his right eye. His mouth felt raw, crusted with clotted blood and his face, stiff and sore. An expression of any kind was difficult.

Quimper said he was going to discharge himself, definitely.

The doctor said that was fine and that the hospital was overcrowded anyway and that Quimper must realise that he was only doing his job in advising Quimper not to discharge himself. If he were Quimper, the doctor said, he would not discharge himself. Definitely.

Quimper said he appreciated the doctor's concern.

The doctor said that was quite all right and would he sign these papers, and if he was fit enough to discharge himself, perhaps he was fit enough to talk to the police, who were cluttering up the emergency room and distracting his nurses.

Quimper said he wouldn't talk to the police. Not till he'd spoken to Detective Superintendent Bridgenorth anyway.

*   *   *

Detective Superintendent Bridgenorth said it was a devil of a lot to ask. Suppressing police inquiries, muzzling press reports, making statements that were only partly true. What Quimper and his friends needed, he said, was a good public relations man, or failing that, they should go and work for a dictator, preferably in a country on the other side of the world.

Quimper said it was a matter of great importance.

"It always is," Bridgenorth said despondently.

"Need to know," Quimper said. It hurt to talk and he could feel the great clot of blood where his teeth had been. "The car caught fire and I swerved into a field."

"You're lucky to be alive," Bridgenorth said, looking at him sternly over the battered briar pipe.

"It was an old car," Quimper said. "It wasn't at all surprising."

*   *   *

Bridgenorth drove the police Hillman stolidly, big hands clamped round the wheel as if they would bend it. "I thought you were liaison," he said looking firmly ahead of him. "I didn't know you were active."

Quimper said, "We're all active some of the time."

"It must get pretty wearing," Bridgenorth said, "especially at your age."

Quimper didn't say anything. He stared at the three-lane carriageway and tried to come to terms with the fact that someone had tried to kill him. Or more precisely, that Harvey Milner had tried to kill him. Harvey Milner or Carruthers. Or someone.

If nobody in the hospital, and nobody who had seen the accident, and none of the policemen who had been involved in the inquiry talked, then it could take whoever it was trying to kill him a day or two to find out what had happened to Quimper. Quimper hoped a day or two would be enough.

Meanwhile he couldn't go back to the Department. He couldn't even go back to his flat.

"Where are you going?" Bridgenorth asked.

Quimper gave him Alistair Hetherset's address.

*   *   *

Alistair Hetherset's flat was on the topmost floor of one of those large houses in Belgravia. Quimper went up white-painted stairs, wheezing. There were modern prints on the landing, blobs and wild splashes of colour that were in accord with the way Quimper felt. Confused.

He paused outside the door and got his breath back. Then, exploratively he leant against the door. The door swung open. Quimper overbalanced into a dim-lit lounge and the sounds of the Rolling Stones at full screech. He fell on to his damaged side and gasped. "Ooooww!" His face was pressed into a sheepskin rug.

The Rolling Stones went *sotto voce*. A girl's voice five feet four inches above him said: "Man! What an entrance!"

Quimper struggled to a sitting position, painfully. He looked up. She was twentyish, freckled, had thick chestnut hair and wide green eyes. She was wearing a long brown dress, like something out of Emily Brontë. She had a pleasant, friendly face and wore no make-up. A chubby, short-fingered hand with unvarnished nails brushed the air in front of Quimper's face.

"Hi!" the girl said. "I'm Cindy."

Quimper took the hand, decided against using it as a lever to get up with and said, "Adrian Carruthers."

Cindy said, "I thought you were Karim. You haven't seen Karim have you?"

"No," Quimper said. "At least I don't think so."

"Oh, you'd know if you'd seen him. He's a big black nigger, all body and afro hairstyle. He's great, you know, cool. Really cool."

"Yes," Quimper said.

"He wants me to go to Algiers." Cindy said, "to meet Eldridge Cleaver."

"That's very nice."

"He's a Black Panther, I think, or a Black Muslim, or something. I never know the difference. Do you?"

"Not at first sight," Quimper admitted.

She looked down at him, suspiciously. "What are you doing here, anyway?"

"I came to see Alistair."

"Alistair isn't here." Cindy smiled. "I am."

Quimper thought about the separate aches in his body and the breath that was just seeping into his lungs. He thought about the Black Panthers or the Black Muslims and decided he'd had enough problems for one day. "Where is Alistair?" he asked.

"He's gone. He's lent me his flat and gone. Isn't it a fantastic pad?"

Peering through the turned down lighting, Quimper saw tables that were plastic cubes and chairs that were globes of brightly-coloured vinyl. Oriental carpets draped the wall and there were sheepskin rugs scattered about the wooden floor.

184

"Yes," Quimper said. "Great." He was thinking that this flat must have cost Alistair nearly £40 a week. It would be interesting to find out how he afforded it on a computer technician's salary.

Cindy asked: "Are you going to sit there all night?"

"No," Quimper said. "I hope not. Do you know where I can find Alistair?"

"Why?" Cindy asked.

Quimper remembered a film he had seen about tough New York policemen and drug pushers. "I'm making a connection," he said.

"Right on the button," Cindy said excitedly. "What you got?"

"I must talk to Alistair," Quimper said.

The girl left him, went to the bedroom and came back, trailing a wisp of acid smoke from a hand-rolled cigarette. She took a long drag, inhaled, and passed the butt to Quimper. "Is it as good as this?" she asked.

Quimper said, "I don't smoke."

The girl looked at him strangely. "You wouldn't have a sample?"

Quimper half-remembered training lectures on narcotics. "No," he said. "But it's Lebanese purple. That's what it is."

Cindy said, "I've never heard of that before."

Quimper said, "It's great. Cool."

Cindy said, "Terrific. For a pusher you look terribly straight."

"If you are a pusher, you have to be."

"But you're sweet. How much have you got?"

Quimper started to shake his head and stopped. "It's for Alistair," he said. "Special consignment."

The girl took another deep drag. "I don't suppose you want to leave it?"

185

"No," Quimper said. "It's more complex than that."

"Bread?" the girl asked. "How much?"

"It's a deal," Quimper said. "Complex. I must get hold of Alistair. Otherwise it's all off."

"He's in Wales," Cindy said.

"Where in Wales?"

She smiled serenely at him. "I haven't the faintest idea. All they said was they were going to Wales and if I wanted to use the flat, I could."

Quimper asked, "Jane went with him?"

"Of course. She always does."

"Why Wales?"

"I haven't the faintest idea."

"When did they go?"

"Three days ago."

"By train?"

"No. They took Jane's car."

"I didn't know Jane had a car."

"She's had a Mini for years."

"I've never seen it," Quimper said.

"It's a funny colour," Cindy said. "Red or purple or something. It's got, you know, basket-weave on the doors and flowers on the roof."

"You wouldn't know the registration number?"

Cindy smiled at him, beatifically. "I haven't the faintest idea," she said.

34

QUIMPER STILL HAD NOWHERE TO GO. So he went to a pub, bought a beer, and thought about not having anywhere to go. Hugh's house in Chelsea was out of the question. He didn't want Hugh involved with people like Carruthers and Milner. As he mentally listed the people he knew, the problem became obvious. There were those like Hugh, whom he couldn't involve, and those who in some way were associated with the Department, and who would be compromised.

Quimper felt alone and very frightened. It was like Beirut. Except then he hadn't been physically hurt. He hadn't had a car explode and roll end over end into a field. In Beirut he had not been in a definite state of shock and suffering from probable concussion.

The question was what to do. Quimper needed money. He needed a place to sleep. The pub would close in about an hour and then he would have to leave. He couldn't risk walking the streets or sleeping on the Embankment. He couldn't risk being questioned by the police. A second beer brought no answers.

For the first time since he had visited Maasten's strip club, Quimper began to regret the impulse that had made him investigate Pute's death. There really had been no need for him to do it. It had been Vivian who had urged him on. He had been foolish to —

Vivian, he thought. *She* had a car. She might even have some money. She was already involved and couldn't get involved any deeper, not if all she did was meet him at the pub.

With a much lightened heart and a nauseous head, Quimper went into the telephone box.

"Quimper!" she cried, when he had told her what he wanted. "How stunningly exciting!" She promised to meet him at the King's Head within the hour. For once, Quimper actually counted the minutes till he saw Vivian.

She barged in, clad in a lightweight blue anorak and green slacks. The pub had already taken on that air of jocular urgency that precedes closing time. Vivian took one look at Quimper and said, "Good heavens!" Before elbowing her way through the crush and getting herself what looked like a triple Scotch.

"Quimper," she said, sitting down opposite him, "what on earth happened?"

"Someone tried to kill me," Quimper said, and shuddered at how dramatic that sounded. The shudder hurt his ribs. "Someone placed a bomb under the bonnet of the Rover," he went on. "An incendiary, operated by a trembler device. The first time I braked hard, it went off."

Vivian took a great gulp of Scotch and said, "Jesus Christ!" She lit a cigarette and asked: "Who?"

Quimper said, "I don't know for certain."

"Are you all right?"

"Just about. I need some money and I need to sleep."

"Oh, Quimper." Vivian took another mouthful of Scotch. "Did you bring the money?" Quimper asked.

"Yes."

"I'd better find a hotel."

Vivian said, "No. It's late, you haven't got any luggage and with a face like you've got, they'll remember you."

Quimper felt sick. The beers on a nearly empty stomach hadn't helped the nausea that accompanied the shock. He was suffering from a kind of delayed reaction and he felt sure that unless he could lie down somewhere very soon he would collapse.

Vivian said, "Of course you could come back to my place. But if anyone's looking for you, that's where they'd probably look first."

Quimper said softly, "I don't want to involve you."

The publican was shouting that it was time and that it had gone ten minutes past.

Vivian said thoughtfully, "We could go to Paul's."

"Who the devil is Paul?"

"Paul is a friend of mine," Vivian said firmly. "We could stay there."

"We?"

"You might need someone to look after you. And believe me, Paul wouldn't."

*　　*　　*

Paul lived in Islington, in one of those narrow, terraced, working-men's houses that had recently become trendy. There was an interesting combination of rustic furniture and padded leather chairs inside, stripped boards and objects that dangled from the ceiling and revolved slowly in the light and made Quimper think he was losing his balance. The walls were painted in single, primitive hues.

Paul was a slim, youngish-looking man with hair that fell to his shoulders. A gold medallion hung in front of his narrow chest, right in the V of his open-necked, black-patterned

189

shirt. He was wearing the tightest pair of yellow trousers that Quimper had seen for a long time.

"Vivian darling," he carolled, kissing Vivian on both cheeks. "How lovely to see you. And is this your friend?" He mouthed a smile at Quimper. "Oh," he said, "you've been fighting."

Vivian introduced them. "Adrian's been in a car accident."

"Dear, dear," Paul said, "how nasty!"

He led them upstairs, into a lounge with red and yellow walls and abstract paintings in the style of Miro. "Anyone like a little drinkie?"

"No, dear," Vivian said, "I must get Adrian to bed."

"Oh!" Paul said, arching his eyebrows and rolling his eyes. "Daring!"

Paul took them up another flight of stairs and threw open the door with a flourish. "There, lovelies," he cried, "it's all yours. And don't do anything I wouldn't do."

The room was small, crammed, most of the space taken up by a large four-poster in the centre of the room. There were two small bookshelves full of paperbacks and a gilt-framed still-life of apples on a table in a dark kitchen.

"I've got to work tomorrow," Paul said. "Going to look at a house in Peterborough. I'll have to leave early." He waved his hands expansively. "But make yourselves at home, lovelies."

"Thanks," Vivian said and kissed him firmly on the cheek. "We will."

Quimper cleared his throat and said, "Thank you, Paul."

After Paul went Quimper walked uneasily around the room and said: "I don't think we should both stay here."

Vivian said, "It's twenty past twelve, Quimper. It will take me an hour to get home and another hour to get in in the morning. Besides, you look terribly ill."

"I feel terribly ill," Quimper said. "And sleeping with you isn't going to make me feel any better."

Vivian laughed. "Don't worry Quimper, I'm not going to take away your innocence."

Quimper fumbled with his jacket and stopped.

"For goodness' sake, Quimper," Vivian cried, "don't be bloody foolish! Or would you prefer to go next door and sleep with Paul?

Vivian left him and went downstairs. Quimper changed and got into bed. He was trying to think about what he should do next when Vivian came back carrying a glass of water and a pill.

"Take this," she said. "It'll help you sleep."

Quimper took the pill. Then, very quickly he told her about his meeting with Mrs. Hetherset and Cindy. There was still a lot to be found out. He began to give Vivian a list of things to do. Buy him a new suit from Burton's, make a check on Alistair Hetherset's flat, try to find out more about the girl, Jane's Mini, find out when Hetherset was expected to return, and if he had told anyone in Records where he was going. Oh yes, could she also write to his insurance company for a claim form . . .

His speech began to slur and there was a warm soothing sensation around his eyes. There were a few more things he wanted Vivian to do, but the light in the room was becoming dim and he had difficulty in focusing. He seemed to be drifting off into a gentle sleep. He fought it weakly. Once he opened his eyes in the darkness.

The last thing he remembered was Vivian climbing into bed beside him and thinking that somehow it was terribly comforting.

35

QUIMPER SURFACED SLOWLY through successive warm layers
of sleep. His mind felt as clear as a bell and the nausea had
vanished. Only a stiff jarring of pain when he tried to move
reminded him of the accident. He lay awake and stared
happily at the ceiling. Vivian had gone and the house was
beautifully silent except for those soft cracking noises that
empty houses make. He must have drifted off to sleep again,
because the next thing he saw was Vivian standing over him,
holding a cup of coffee. "It's Moroccan," she said, "but quite
good."

Quimper took it gratefully. "What time is it?"

"Twenty past twelve." Vivian was still wearing the slacks
and the anorak of the previous night. "How do you feel?"

"Fine."

Vivian lit a cigarette. "I've got most of the information
you wanted."

"Good girl!"

"The flat is leased to Hetherset's girlfriend. Her name's
Jane Brewster. She works as a secretary in an advertising
agency and the flat is paid for by her ex-husband. She is
divorced."

Quimper sipped the coffee slowly, relishing the way the

liquid trickled down his throat and hit his stomach in a warm wave. "How did you find that out?" he asked.

"Simple," Vivian said. "The rates people. It's astonishing how much they'll tell you if you ask nicely." Vivian pulled out a notepad and looked at it. "Her car is a Mini, 2216CD. It's registered as red, but people don't always notify the RMV of change of colour."

"No," Quimper agreed. "Not if they paint flowers on it."

"Hetherset moved in with Mrs. Brewster six months ago. He hasn't notified the Department of his change of address."

"Interesting," said Quimper.

"And they are in Cardiganshire."

"How do you know?"

"I phoned her office," Vivian said. "I said I was a friend of Jane's, flew in this minute from New York and gee, how Jane and I had always been such close friends and I was going to stay with her and how I liked little old London and all those lovely soldiers with white tasselled hats." Vivian laughed. "They fell for it. They were as helpful as possible. Someone remembered that Jane had a place somewhere in Wales, somewhere in Cardiganshire."

"Cardiganshire is a big county," Quimper said.

Vivian shrugged. "I did what I could. Now there's food for you in the dining room and a smart brown suit from Burton's. I must get back to the office. So you just rest up till I come back and we'll plan what we're going to do next."

* * *

Quimper couldn't let it wait that long. He went downstairs and ate and had a look at the suit and decided the brown was too bright. It made him look like a car salesman.

Vivian had also bought some shirts and socks, handkerchiefs, underwear and even a couple of ties. Quimper began to think that Vivian was a real jewel.

He took the clothes back to his room, pottered down to the lounge, picked up a telephone and called a high official in the constabulary of Cardiganshire. It was a matter of importance and of discretion, Quimper said. They were looking for two people in a purple Mini, 2216CD. No, they didn't want them arrested or anything. All they wanted to know was where they were staying.

The high official in the constabulary of Cardiganshire added Quimper's request on to the list of things he had to do, and said he would call back as soon as his men found something. Quimper was profuse in his thanks. In passing he mentioned that he was not at his office, and could the high official in the constabulary of Cardiganshire remember to call him at a different number. The high official was glad to co-operate. He made a note of Paul's telephone number.

*   *   *

An hour later, Vivian was back, pounding up the stairs like a runaway cannon ball. "Quimper!" she cried, "Quimper! Where are you?" She burst into the room, face spread apart in a wide, beaming grin. "I know where they are," she said breathlessly. "They are in a cottage about three miles from a village called Pen-y-garn.

Quimper put down the Simenon he was reading and tried to appear as phlegmatic as that legendary Frenchman's most famous character, Maigret. "Pardon," he said.

"The Department's got a file on Jane Brewster," Vivian said. "I had Kumar do a printout for me. She owns a small cottage near Pen-y-garn."

"Why does the Department have a file on Jane Brewster?"

"Member of suspect organisation."

194

"What organisation?"

"They sound like a crowd of circus motorcyclists," Vivian said. "They call themselves the Red Gnomes."

Quimper stood up, all phlegm gone now. "Could you," he asked excitedly, "hire me a car?"

"Don't need to," Vivian said. "We can go in mine."

"But —"

"No buts, Adrian. You aren't fit to drive a long distance and besides the Department still owes me six and a half days' casual leave."

*   *   *

Two hours later Quimper was seated awkwardly in the jumpseat of Vivian's blue MG Midget and they were streaking up the M4 at a highly illegal speed. The noise from the exhaust made prolonged conversation impossible, and drowned the radio. Quimper eyed the speedometer nervously. "There's a speed limit," he shouted.

"Made by fools for even bigger fools," she replied cheerily and pressed on.

They streaked past family saloons cluttering up the centre carriageway and huge trucks grinding slowly up the inside lane. Quimper decided that the best thing he could do under the circumstances was watch the slow lane for cruising police cars.

"Why did you leave the police, Adrian?"

The wind was tearing round the screen with a hard clattering noise.

Quimper shouted. "Because of a gangster called Scallo." It was the first time he had told anyone about it, except Hugh.

"Who?"

Quimper spelt it out for her. "Italian," he said.

"You mean like the Mafia. That must have been exciting."

"He wasn't in the Mafia. Scallo was simply a thug with too many people in authority on his payroll. I wanted to get him and the only way I could do that was by working alone." Quimper stopped. The shouting was hurting his throat. He shouted: "Can you slow down? The shouting is hurting my throat."

Vivian nipped smartly into the centre lane, right across the path of an overloaded Cortina Estate. The exhaust roar settled down to a quiet burble. The wind noise died to a discreet whisper. Quimper said, "Working alone was a mistake. But at the time there was no alternative. I didn't know who was being paid by Scallo and who wasn't. The only way I could find out was by taking graft too."

"What did you do with the money?"

"Gave it away mostly, to charities and that. Someone, perhaps even Scallo suspected what I was at. They tipped off the rubber heels — the policemen who check on other policemen."

They passed a rest area, ugly, crowded, soulless buildings of concrete and glass, smelling of greasy food and petrol.

"Fortunately, I had enough evidence by then. I took Scallo with me." Quimper laughed. "They needed my evidence to convict Scallo so they couldn't afford to have me publicly discredited. We reached an agreement. After Scallo was convicted, I agreed to resign."

Vivian said, "But that's unfair, Adrian, you shouldn't have let them do it."

"Life's unfair, Vivian. Sometimes harsh judgments are made. One must learn to live with them."

Vivian snorted and gunned the car angrily into the fast lane. "If you believe that," she shouted above the exhaust roar, "you're too damned soft to survive."

*   *   *

They reached Pen-y-garn six hours later. It was a tiny village reached through narrow winding roads, guarded by high banks. There was a tobacconist and an ironmonger, a butcher and a grocer who also sold bread. There was one pub which had one spare room for guests.

That night Adrian Quimper did not sleep very much or very well. But he was more relaxed the next morning — far more relaxed.

36

THE HIGH OFFICIAL in the constabulary of Cardiganshire had quite a long list. A speed boat had overturned in the bay, a truck full of chemicals had gone off the road near Tal Sarn and was leaking chemicals into the River Aeron, Nationalists had obliterated all the signposts around Lampeter and an Electricity Board helicopter checking for illicit tapping of power had somehow contrived to land on the edge of Tregaron Bog. The latest reports were that the helicopter was sinking slowly.

The next day the helicopter had sunk and the official's list was even longer.

Being a neat sort of person he made out a fresh list and threw away the old one. It was only after the purple Mini had been traced that he remembered there had been a telephone number on the old list. It wasn't, however, important. He remembered the coding Quimper had used when asking for his assistance. Because they usually had very little to do with each other he took some time to find the telephone number of the Department. By the time he got through to London, the man Quimper was out.

The high official in the constabulary of Cardiganshire was however equal to the occasion. He left the information

Quimper wanted with an intelligent sounding young lady, who assured him that it would reach the right quarter without delay.

*   *   *

The pub was dark, cosy, all deep brown and thick glass, furnished with upright puritan chairs, with red padding Quimper drank beer and sat by the doorway where he could see part of the village street. Vivian drank sherry and read *The Cricketer.*When he wasn't thinking about the reason why they were in Pen-y-garn Quimper felt quite peaceful.

It was just after noon when the purple Mini with the basket-weave doors and the flowers on the roof edged down the street and stopped at the tobacconists. Quimper saw a tall fair-haired man get out, go into the tobacconists and come out a few minutes later carrying a parcel which he dropped on to the rear seat of the car. The Mini moved away from the tobacconists and came down the street. It turned into the courtyard of the pub.

Quimper left his post by the door, walked to the rear of the pub, and out into the yard behind it. He went round the back of the pub and re-entered it through the swing doors of the public bar.

Hetherset and the girl were standing at the counter. Their drinks were in front of them, a pint of bitter for him and a gin and tonic for her. "Alistair!" Quimper cried.

Hetherset turned. He was quite tall, over six feet and he had a round, good-looking innocent kind of face with blond hair parted from the side and wide-apart blue eyes. Although he was in his mid thirties, he still looked boyish with all the immaturity and weakness that boyishness implies. Hetherset raised a hand to his roll-neck sweater. It was one of those

199

thin woollen things that hugged the body and revealed the soft curve of Hetherset's belly.

"Adrian Quimper," Hetherset said slowly. "Well, well."

He turned to the girl and said : "Darling, this is Adrian Quimper. He works for the Department."

The girl glared hostilely at Quimper. She had a strong-chinned, narrow face that was made to look smaller by the untidy mass of brown hair that hung to her shoulders. She wore a blue denim outfit, a short, faded military-style jacket and jeans.

Quimper said, "Fancy meeting you here."

The girl said, "Alistair isn't working now, Mr. Quimper. He's away from your blasted computers, so whatever you do don't talk shop."

Alistair smiled hesitantly. "Jane darling, Mr. Quimper doesn't work on computers. Mr. Quimper is in Security. Isn't that right?"

"Yes," Quimper said. "I saw your mother yesterday."

"That old bitch," Jane said.

"Darling —"

"She's quite well," Quimper said. "Tells me you once wanted to be a painter."

"Didn't you ever want to be anything?" Alistair asked, stung.

"Or do you like snooping?" Jane asked. "Isn't that what Security is all about?"

Quimper sighed and looked down at his glass. "Anyone for another drink?"

"No," Jane snapped.

Quimper looked directly at Alistair. "It's been a long time since school," he said. "I didn't know you were in the Department until the other day."

Alistair took a gulp at his beer and said, "I'll have a half, in there."

Quimper moved up to the bar and ordered the drinks.

"What happened to your face?" Jane asked. "Got it caught in someone's bedroom door?" She laughed loudly at her own joke.

Quimper waited for her to stop. "I was in a car smash."

"Bad?" Alistair asked.

"The car's a write off."

"What were you doing? Running away from someone?"

"No," Quimper said. "Not really." He looked at the narrow-set eyes framed by the strands of untidy brown hair. "You're being damn rude," he said, "and there's no reason for it."

"What are you going to do about it, dad?" she asked. "I'm too big to be spanked."

Quimper turned to Alistair, "I'd like a word with you. In private."

Jane said, "Alistair is not working for you now, Mr. Quimper. You can say anything you like to him in front of me."

Quimper said. "It would be better if we could talk —"

Jane cried, "Or you'll take him down to some police station and work him over with rubber truncheons. Is that it Mr. Quimper? Is that it?"

"We don't use rubber truncheons any more," Quimper said. "Now we give electric shocks to the genitals."

She smiled at him over the top of her glass. "I think the police are wonderful."

Quimper could cheerfully have smashed the glass against her tobacco-stained teeth.

"So you were just passing through," Alistair asked.

Quimper shook his head. "If it were anyone else, I'd be

just passing through. But we have a few things in common, Alistair —"

"Cut the bullshit, Quimper," Jane said. "Don't flannel us. We know you and your kind too well for that."

Quimper kept looking at Alistair. "I came specially to see you."

"How did you know where I was?"

"Snooping," Jane cried. "Interfering with privacy. Sneaking around. You don't have to answer his stupid questions, Alistair."

Quimper said, "It isn't important how I found out. The important thing is that I am here, and we must talk."

Jane said, "We've got nothing to say to you, copper."

"Alistair, some tapes you were working on are missing from Records. They are important tapes. The back-up information has also been lost."

Alistair smiled. "I'm only an operator," he said. "I don't deal with storage."

"But you know about the tapes, don't you Alistair?"

Alistair looked away. Jane swallowed her drink and slammed her glass on the bar counter. "Let's go, Alistair," she said. "I'm hungry and this place is beginning to smell like a pigsty."

Quimper let them go. He knew where they lived, and his experience told him that they wouldn't make a run for it. No, it wouldn't take much to wear Alistair down. All Quimper had to do was to be there and to let Alistair know he was there. Alistair's conscience would do the rest.

But that was before the yellow Porsche growled into the courtyard of the pub, and Harvey Milner stepped out.

37

Milner stood there for a moment, lean and spare, weak shadow rectilineal across the pounded-up earth. He tugged his jacket straight and walked into the pub.

"What the hell are you doing here?" he asked Quimper.

Quimper rested his beer on the counter. "One might well ask you the same question, Harvey," he replied mildly and looked away.

"Carruthers took you off the job two days ago," Milner said. "What are you doing here?"

"Enjoying," Vivian said from behind Quimper, "what is vulgarly known as a dirty weekend."

"It isn't a weekend," Milner snapped.

Quimper suppressed a smile, "We couldn't wait," he said.

Milner thrust his face at Quimper. "Comedian are you? Well you'd better get back to London fast. Because you've got no kind of business here."

"Harvey," Quimper said. "Why don't you have a drink?"

"Don't drink," Harvey said, taking his face away.

Quimper noticed that Milner hadn't asked any questions about the bruises on his own face.

"You'd better get back to London," Milner said. "Now."

"That sounds like an order, Harvey."

"Dead right, it is."

Quimper gave him a frosty smile. "May I remind you, Harvey," he said, "that I am a section head. *You* don't give me orders."

"Maybe. But as far as I'm concerned you're a nothing. Get that. Nothing. And I'm telling you to get the hell out of here."

Quimper asked, "Are you worried I'll find the tapes first?"

Milner laughed nastily. "You couldn't find — what do you call it — Big Ben if it fell on your head."

"We'll see, Harvey," Quimper said, quietly. "We'll see."

Milner asked, "Has Hetherset been here?"

Quimper hesitated. "Yes."

"You speak to him?"

"Yes," Quimper said. "We've known each other for some time. We attended the same school."

"What kind of school was that? Something run by the KGB?"

"No," Quimper said. "Actually it was run by my father. In Devon."

Milner snorted. "Was he a Commie too?"

"No," Quimper said. "As a matter of fact he voted Tory."

Milner shrugged. "All right. Get back to London. Both of you."

"And leave Hetherset to you?"

"That's right."

"In that case," Quimper said, "A word of advice. Don't rush Hetherset. You'll only scare him. He's got to be led along. It would be best if I were to talk to him. He trusts me."

"I bet he does."

"Look," Quimper said. "I don't give a damn which of us gets the credit for this job. The important thing is to get the tapes back. If you leave Hetherset to me, he'll give up the tapes — if he has them. I'll guarantee that."

"No deal," Milner said. "You're out Quimper. Out and over the hill and forgotten. You're a has-been. So why don't you shift your arse back to London. You're only getting in the way."

"I'm not taking orders from you," Quimper snapped.

"I wouldn't bet on that," Milner said.

Quimper asked, "What are you going to do? Start waving your gun around?"

"Maybe."

Quimper asked, "Have you considered that I might be carrying a gun too?"

Milner laughed. It was a sneering, insulting laugh, hardly six inches from Quimper's face. "You couldn't use a gun, Quimper, not if your life depended on it." His eyes flickered over Quimper. "Besides, you haven't got a gun," he said.

"How do you know I wouldn't use one, if I had one?"

"Because I know all about Beirut," Milner said. He stepped closer to Quimper. "You're shit scared, Quimper. It stands out a mile. Now if it had been me in Beirut I'd never have let that bastard get away."

"No," Quimper said quietly. His body had grown quite rigid. He remembered Pute's printout. The Beirut incident was not part of his personal file.

Milner said. "You're either shit scared or you're a Commie. Either way don't try gun talk on me. I've got you sized up, right up to there."

Quimper moved a couple of paces back. "Really?"

"Really. Now be sensible and get the hell out of here."

"All right Harvey," Quimper said. He started to move past Milner, leaving the bar ahead of Vivian. Right in front of Milner he stopped and turned.

"Harvey," Quimper said and held up his right hand, shoulder high.

"What?" Milner leaned forward to see what was in Quimper's right palm.

Quimper waited till Milner's head was clear of his body and hit him on the point of the jaw. It was a short, sharp, vicious left hook delivered from hardly twelve inches away. It was travelling quickly and had a hundred and seventy-five pounds behind it when it connected. Milner's eyes went glassy, his knees buckled.

Quimper stepped forward and caught Milner before he fell. Quickly he laid him out on the floor of the pub. He knelt down, opened Milner's jacket and took out the Colt Combat Commander. Then he stood up and looked across at the bar-man. "It's all right," he said, "it's for a bet. We're friends, really." He dropped two five-pound-notes on the counter. "Come on," he said to Vivian. "Let's take Harvey's advice and get the hell out of here."

38

Vivian hurled the mg Midget along tight little Welsh lanes, raggedly. The car bounced and rolled, engine blaring in third. Once they skidded on a patch of mud, throwing into a slow, silent, snake-like slide, scrubbing gravel inches from the banks that bordered the road.

Jane Brewster's cottage was about three miles from the pub. It was reached by a steep narrow drive, at the end of which the purple Mini was parked. The cottage was small, white, with a slate roof, once used by farm labourers.

"I'm going in alone," Quimper said. "Get the car out of sight, around the corner."

"But Adrian —"

Quimper was already out of the car and running up the drive. His ribs ached as his lungs sucked in air. Once, he slipped.

He reached the door and pounded on it. Jane's untidy head appeared round its edge. "You're not coming in here," she said.

Quimper shouldered the door into her face.

She cried out and reeled back, off balance. Quimper pushed into the cottage. Almost at once Jane came at him, fingers stiffened into claws. "You've no right!" she shouted. Quimper slapped her viciously across the face twice.

She gasped and bent down, hands pressed to her stinging face. "Bastard," she sobbed, "pig."

"Complain about me to your M.P.," Quimper cried and rushed into the dim-lit lounge. "Alistair!" he shouted. "Alistair!"

Alistair was in a small room at the back that had been converted into a studio by means of skylights and what, if they had been large enough, would have been called French windows. Easels loaded with unfinished canvases leant against white walls. In the centre of the room was another easel and another unfinished painting. Beside it, on a small high table, was a mass of pots and paints and brushes and tubes. Alistair was sitting astride a straight backed chair a few feet away from the easel. His chest was pressed against the back rest and his arms dangled from it. His face was pale and there was a pinched, hunted look about his eyes and mouth.

"Adrian," he said tremulously.

"Where are the tapes, Alistair? You've got to tell me."

Alistair looked blank eyed at his painting.

"I don't know what you are talking about," he said.

"Alistair," Quimper cried, "they know. They've sent someone after you to get them."

Jane pushed into the room. Her eyes were swollen with tears and her face was red striped by Quimper's fingers. There was a bruise above her eyebrow where the door had caught her.

"Bastard!" she screamed at Quimper. "Pig! You haven't even got a search warrant."

Quimper marvelled at the mentality that could preach anarchy and yet when attacked, scream so loudly for the protection of the law. "Shut up," he said abruptly.

She began to whimper. "Alistair, see what he's done to me. No one's done that to me before."

"Adrian, did you —"

"Yes," Quimper snapped. Once more he was back in the jungle. Once more he was where only the fittest to survive, did. He thought they were too young to know what that was about. It was easy to become a flower person, if you hadn't known war. "Alistair," he said, "there's a man on his way up here. He wants the tapes. He will have no hesitation in killing you to get them."

"Rubbish," Jane said. "This is England. This is a civilised country."

Quimper wasn't prepared to argue either statement with her. "Give me the tapes, Alistair, please."

Alistair's mouth tightened. "Haven't got them," he said. "Now get out."

"He hit me," Jane said. "Throw him out, Alistair."

Alistair looked hesitant.

"There isn't bloody time," Quimper cried. "They've sent Harvey Milner after you. The man who killed Pute."

"Pute's dead?"

"Yes. See this." Quimper pointed to his own face. "That's the result of a bomb in my car."

"Lies," Jane cried, "all bloody lies."

"Alistair, I'll do whatever I can to help you. I promise that. Just give me the tapes and let's get out of here before Milner comes."

"We aren't going to run," Jane said.

Quimper showed Alistair the torn knuckles of his left fist. "I had to hit Milner, to delay him. We haven't got much time."

Alistair asked, "What did you mean then, Adrian, about helping me?"

209

"I'll do what I can."

"You stupid fool!" Jane cried. "Don't believe him! He's a policeman!"

Quimper said to Alistair. "You know what I really am. Nevertheless, I promise you, I'll do everything I can to help you. Damn it, Alistair, we owe the old school something!"

"I always liked you at school, Adrian. Even though you were much older. You used to bat very straight, I remember."

"Yes," Quimper said. "Yes, yes. And I promise you I've laid it on the line with you. I'll help you. Only, for God's sake, tell me where the tapes are."

"I don't know how you can do what you're doing, Adrian," Alistair said. "This stinking, filthy job of yours, bursting into houses, beating up women, snooping, spying, for what? To protect a tatty little secret department. A place that has no name and no personality."

"Do you know what they've got in Records, Adrian? Files. Files on people. People who've never done anything wrong. People who are only suspected of doing something wrong. How would you like to be found guilty by suspicion, Adrian?"

"Is that what you feared would happen to the Red Gnomes?" Quimper asked. He looked directly at Alistair. "Or were you frightened that someone in Records would find out you were a member?"

"It wasn't that," Alistair said and stopped.

Quimper said softly, "So you did take them after all."

Alistair's knuckles whitened on the back of the chair. He stared fixedly at the stone floor. "Yes," he said. "I took the tapes."

"You stupid, stupid fool!" Jane cried.

Quimper asked. "How did you get the tapes out?"

"I was on the dead shift. Ten to six. It's only routine. There were only two of us."

"And Kumar was late and Pute left early. You knew that would happen?"

Alistair nodded. "All I had to do was walk in, open the safe and take the tapes. I kept them in my briefcase and walked out with them the next morning." He smiled. "No one checks us coming off the dead shift."

"Who was it," Quimper asked, "who told you the combination? Who was it who arranged for Kumar to be late?"

Alistair looked up at Quimper and gave him a tired smile. "I'm not telling you that," he said.

Quimper asked, "What's happened to the tapes?"

"They're safe. All that was required was that they be kept out of circulation for a few days."

"Why?"

"So that we — they — the Red Gnomes would have time to reorganise."

"You damned idiot," Jane snapped. "You could get twenty years for telling him this."

Alistair shook his head. "No," he said and repeated. "No. I haven't committed any crime. The tapes have only been borrowed. No one else has seen them. Soon the tapes will be returned, intact." He looked up at Quimper. "If you steal you must have an intention to keep, mustn't you?"

"This is a lot more serious than stealing," Quimper said.

"Is it, Adrian? Why?"

"For a start you are in breach of the Official Secrets Act."

"I haven't given any secrets away."

"You're helping a subversive organisation."

Alistair laughed. "There's nothing subversive about the Gnomes. They're just a harmless bunch of kids who want to live their own lives. Just because they want none of your scheming and politics and infamy it doesn't mean they are subversive. All they want is peace and to end ugliness and evil and the sham you people make.

"That's why I took the tapes. To protect them and because Pute had placed them on a suspect list, without reason, only because *he* thought they were dangerous. All I wanted to do was stop them from being investigated and harassed." Alistair looked up at Quimper. "You know, Adrian, there are some of us who want a better world, where there are no poor, and no under-privileged, and young men aren't sent to places like Vietnam to keep the armaments makers in profit."

"That's hippie, drop-out talk," Harvey Milner said from the doorway. His jaw was red and swollen and he stood there, lithe and erect in his rubber-soled, handmade casuals. He was carrying a stubby black Derringer, the kind that was chambered for the .38 Special.

Quimper cursed silently. He should have remembered that Milner was a professional, that professionals usually carried back-up guns.

Milner moved into the room and shut the door behind him. He waved the gun at Quimper. "Over against the wall, you," he said. "And keep your hands where I can see them."

Quimper did as he was told. From where he stood, Milner quite easily covered the three of them. "All right punk," he said to Alistair, "where are the tapes?"

Alistair sat white-faced. His lips moved but no words came out.

"Hurry up, punk. I've got no time to waste."

Alistair said, "I'm not telling you."

Milner stepped up to the easel that was in the centre of the room. "Painting," he said. "Nice." Then he picked up the paint scraper and ripped a long jagged X in the canvas.

"You foul, insensitive turd!" Jane screamed and leaped at him. "Leave us al —"

Milner fired. The bullet caught her in mid-air. Her body crashed with outflung arms against the easel. The back of her faded blue denim jacket charred and erupted blood.

Alistair moaned. "You've killed her, you swine. You've killed her."

"Yes," Milner said. He was back in place, gun covering both of them.

Horrified, Quimper watched the blood seep out of Jane's clothing. Milner had got her through the heart. It was damned good shooting and then he remembered where he was and what he was supposed to be doing. Jane lay on the floor, white-faced, cheek pressed to the unfinished canvas, her hair spread all around it.

Milner said to Alistair, "All right punk, where are the tapes?"

Alistair was moving towards Jane, with unseeing eyes, blinded by tears that rolled down his cheeks. "They're in the lounge," he sobbed. "Under the sofa."

It was as simple as that, Quimper thought.

Then Milner shot Alistair. The report echoed in the tiny room. Alistair whirled, loose-armed, crashed against the chair, fell.

Quimper started to move, hand darting towards the pocket where he had kept Milner's Colt. His palm stopped round the butt, pulled. The barrel twisted in his clothing, stuck.

Milner turned. Ugly black barrel and bright yellow flash, the sound of the shot filling Quimper's ears. Quimper whirled. He spun round, cannoned into the wall, rolled along it and hit the floor. He could smell the cordite on his clothes and there was a great glob of pain high on the left side of his chest. Black handmade moccasins spread easily apart on the dusty floor. There was a ball of cellophane paper resting between them, bisected by a narrow red stripe. Very clearly Quimper saw Milner standing above him, arm extended, taking careful aim.

Quimper twisted. His right hand was still trapped in his pocket, the gun still trapped in his clothing. Quimper fired.

A great gaping hole flared in the middle of Milner's body. Globules of blood and shreds of yellow flesh flew wetly through the air. The Derringer clattered from Milner's hand and Milner kicked over backwards and fell. He lay there twitching, gasped once and then went still.

Slowly Quimper got up. Very slowly. The bullet had smashed through the base of the pectoral muscle and jammed against the shoulder blade. It hurt him to breathe. He could feel the wetness trickling down his arm, sticking on to his shirt, running along cold nerveless fingers and trickling to the floor. He was still standing there dazed when Vivian came in.

39

VIVIAN HAD A FIRST AID KIT in the car. It wasn't much help against a bullet wound, but at least she managed to wad the injury and staunch the bleeding.

"I'll have to get you to a doctor," she said.

Quimper let his head loll. "No," he said weakly. "No doctors." Doctors would mean reports, the police, inquiries, delays. There was no time to be wasted. "London," Quimper said. "My brother, Hugh."

He gave her the address.

"London's miles away," Vivian said.

"Drive quickly," Quimper said and smiled.

An hour later the pain started, deep, probing, insistent. It cut through his body like a knife. Quimper began to sweat and he forced his teeth against his lips to stifle the cries of agony. Wind shrieked past them, the exhaust roared. His tongue felt dry and heavy and swollen and there was a slow heavy drum beat in his head like a funeral tattoo. He felt heat seep through the wound-up window. Saw a sky that was glaringly blue. Each time his body rolled with the movement of the car there was a sharp stab of pain.

He slept or went unconscious for a time. There was heat all around him and pain, always the pain that started at his shoulder and spread through his body, the pain that cut through him, steel-tipped, the pain that compressed his chest and dried his mouth and made him cry out.

Then later, hours later, there was Hugh, anxious, concerned and Noelene, stiff-lipped, silent. Later there was the sharp jab of a needle and the long teetering walk up the steps, the impossible climb on to the high bed in Hugh's surgery.

"How is it?" Hugh was asking, smiling a reassurance that reached his eyes.

"Better." The morphine was beginning to take effect.

Hugh was peeling away the blood-soaked wadding. "You'd better work union hours."

"Some other time," Quimper said. "Later."

"It's clean," Hugh said. "But you've lost a lot of blood. You're weak."

"Hugh, I can't go into hospital. There's something I have to do."

"There's time. Afterwards."

Quimper tried to sit up. "Don't," Hugh said, "you'll start the bleeding again."

Quimper lay still. "Hugh, don't put me to sleep. Give me something to carry on. It's damned important."

Hugh's eyes looked down into his. "Is anything that important, Adrian?"

"This time it is. And I'm the only one." He had to laugh. "The only one."

Hugh moved away, busied himself with stainless-steel kidney dishes and probes. There was a strong smell of rectified spirit.

"How much time have you got?"

"Not much," Quimper said.

"Can you spare three hours to sleep?"

216

"I think so."

Hugh came back squirting a syringe, checking for air bubbles. Quimper said : "Hugh, promise me it'll only be three hours."

Hugh smiled sadly. "Promise," he said. "Scout's word of honour."

He felt Hugh's hand take his arm. For a while Hugh waited. It was like being back in college, Adrian thought, being with Hugh, feeling him near, knowing that everything was going to be all right.

Quimper slept.

＊　　　＊　　　＊

He came awake thick-headed, nauseous. Hugh was still there. There were lights on in the surgery and he was holding out a glass. "Drink this."

Quimper drank. It cleared his mouth, took away the taste of scum. His shoulder felt better, stiffer, clean. The pain had receded to a dull throb.

"How much time do you need?" Hugh asked, holding his watch before Quimper's eyes.

"About five, six hours."

"I'll give you something," Hugh said. "Only if you'll promise to come back here."

"I'm not sure," Quimper said. "It might not be — "

"I'll be waiting," Hugh said and rapidly placed some pills on Adrian's tongue.

＊　　　＊　　　＊

Vivian was still there talking to Noelene. Vivian stared at him uncomprehendingly. Quimper smiled. "We'd better go," he said and added inconsequentially. "I'm sorry."

Noelene asked, "Adrian, are you all right? Are you sure you should be going out?"

"I'm sure," Quimper said.

Whatever Hugh had given him had cleared his head. His body felt brimful of energy and there was hardly any pain. Outside, huddled in the MG Midget, he asked Vivian: "How well do you know Mr. Kumar?"

"Reasonably," she said.

"Think you could ask him a favour?"

Vivian nodded.

"Right. Let's go there."

He stayed in the car while Vivian went up to the flat and spoke to Kumar. A few minutes afterwards she was back. "He says he'll follow us," she said. "In his own car."

Quimper hoped someone hadn't stolen Kumar's battery.

40

THEY LEFT BOTH CARS in the square round the corner from the Department and walked the few yards to it. Not speaking they went down in the lift to Records, Quimper keeping his injured shoulder away from the steel sides of the lift and his companions. Kumar signed them in and they went through the flat-lit machine room into his office.

Vivian dumped the green and gold Harrods' carrier bag on the desk. "The Kiriov tapes," she said.

Kumar opened the bag and took out the tapes, holding them flat on their sides. "How did you — "

"Later," Quimper said. "First you'd better check them for damage."

"It'll mean doing a printout, Mr. Quimper."

"That's all right," Quimper said and sat down.

"I'm not sure — "

"I have the authority," Quimper said flatly. "Go on, please. We haven't much time."

Kumar picked up the tapes and went out. They heard him moving in the machine room outside and soon afterwards there was a subdued clattering, like a muted machine-gun.

Vivian lit a cigarette. "How do you feel, Adrian?" she asked.

"Fine," Quimper said, thinking that he needed to learn one thing more before he knew who had asked Alistair Hetherset to remove the tapes.

*　　*　　*

Bridgenorth shifted uncomfortably in the swivel chair with the loose socket and puffed his pipe defiantly at David Carruthers. "It must be true," he said, "I mean, it's the only logical explanation, isn't it?"

David Carruthers stared impassively at Bridgenorth. He was seated sideways to the broad desk, whose wood and leather was scarred by ink stains and smouldering cigarettes. "Is that why you wanted me here? In your office?"

Bridgenorth nodded. "I believe there is a spy in your Department," he said.

"Give me your reasons, again," Carruthers said.

"First there was the government car," Bridgenorth said. "A black Humber Imperial was seen outside the flats the night Amory and Kiriov were killed."

"Who saw it?"

"A little boy living on the fourth floor. He described the car to me with great accuracy."

Carruthers looked sceptical.

"Then there was the gun," Bridgenorth said. "A Browning. One of ours. Standard British Army issue."

"Lots of Germans used Brownings in the last war," Carruthers said. "They were made in Belgium after all."

"Amory and Kiriov were shot at close range," Bridgenorth said. "Must have been someone who was known to Amory, someone who knew the code. Otherwise Amory would never have let him into the flat."

Carruthers said, "Yes, there's that."

After a while Bridgenorth said, "You'll have to do something about it now. I mean it's your responsibility."

Carruthers looked thoughtfully at Bridgenorth. "I suppose," he said, "I'll have to do something."

*　　*　　*

The mottled white strip of paper flowed over the desk in a turgid stream. It contained the sediment of espionage, names, addresses, lists of people, of organisations, all neatly classified, capable of this interpretation or that, information, the basis for research and investigation and surveillance.

At the top of the printout was a list of forty-two names, all Russian, all working for the Soviet Trade Delegation. Each of the forty-two persons was described as a specialist in a particular industry. Then followed the names of twenty-seven 'contract examiners' who were in reality KGB operatives.

After that there came a short statement of information that the Russians needed. Information on electronics. On transformers, on zena diodes and computer circuitry. The operating manual of BOADICEA, BOAC's forty-two million-pound computerised seat reservation system was especially valuable. The Russians lacked information and experience of very large computers and the very large programs that could be run on them.

Then came a long list of all the major companies involved in these industries, the office bearers and key technical personnel. There was a separate list of those people who had at some time been known to, or could possibly have, however innocently, met with the Russians. A KGB man who was an ardent supporter of the Ministry of Defence football team accounted for no less than seventy names.

Then the printout moved to harder fact. People who were

known to have been contacted, people who were suspected of being contacted. Lists of people belonging to suspect organisations and a list of people who were members of subversive organisations and who worked in these industries.

The information was endless. Classification after classification, sub-classification, analysis, division, tying up a technician in an electronic systems factory with a staff sergeant who had access on information on classified weaponry, with a Russian aide for cultural affairs, with a statistician who now lived in France.

"There's more," Kumar said excitedly. "A whole lot more. There's something on how the information on a new fighter is being leaked."

"There always is," Quimper said and looked up at Kumar. "I want a printout on Harvey Milner. And on these three people."

Kumar looked at the list and laughed. "Milner is OK, Mr. Quimper. But these others. What are you doing? One of them is dead and the others haven't been heard of for years."

"I know," Quimper said and quoted "Time present and time past are both perhaps contained in time future. And time future contained in time present." He did not know why he said it. He must have been delirious.

"That's T. S. Eliot," Kumar said. "Ash Wednesday."

It was actually Burnt Norton, the first of the *Four Quartets,* but Quimper didn't say anything. While Kumar went away to get the information he sent Vivian upstairs with an authorisation for a gun, a Smith and Wesson Airweight model with a full load of .38 magnum cartridge.

Vivian came back before Kumar did and left the gun on the table. Picking up a sheet of paper, Quimper began to write a letter. He headed it, "To whom it may concern" and below that, awkwardly, because of his wounded shoulder, he wrote his resignation.

Kumar came in carrying the printed sheets. Quimper hardly looked at them. "Mr. Kumar," he said, "I need three more."

He told Kumar what printouts he needed.

Kumar swallowed nervously. "I can't do that, Mr. Quimper. I have no authority. You have not the authority, either."

Quimper picked up the Smith and Wesson. "I have," he said, darkly. He looked at Vivian. "Can you operate those machines?"

"If I have to."

"You can't," Kumar cried. "You'll break them!"

"So," Vivian said equably.

"You can tell them it was me," Quimper said to Kumar. "That I forced you. I am forcing you."

Kumar sighed. "I thought you were a nice man, Mr. Quimper," he said, and added: "Put that gun away." He glared balefully at Vivian. "I'm never going anywhere with you," he said, "or doing you any more favours."

* * *

Carefully Quimper compared the two batches of printout. One from the second batch he discounted immediately. It was the wrong age group. He studied the others for a while longer and when he'd finished, he knew. He couldn't prove anything, but he knew.

In the second batch there was one printout that was almost identical with the first three. The life story of a man who had been at Trinity College, Cambridge, from 1926 to 1931, who had worked on *The Times* from 1934 to 1937, a man who had been a leading member of the Anglo-German Fellowship from 1934 until it was rapidly wound up in September, 1939.

The man whose life story he was reading had been brilliant, distinguished, a tribute to the greatness of his people. From journalism he had gone to intelligence and then to diplomacy. He had worked with Section D of the SIS, been responsible for liaison with the CIA, had even worked with the British Embassy in Washington from 1947 to 1949.

He had returned to England, full of power. He had been able to suppress reports of drunken orgies in Alexandria and wild parties in Tangier and Gibraltar.

In May 1951 he'd had the power to warn. In May 1951 he had initiated that incongruous journey that kept the press on tenterhooks through the last week of that month, a journey that began with the hire of a cream Austin A70 from a garage in Wigmore Street and the purchase of a new suitcase and mackintosh from a Bond Street clothing store, a journey that left one Mr. Hewitt wondering why his friend had not stopped to say goodbye, whose destination and purpose was only made conclusive some five years later, on February 11th, 1956, when Donald Maclean and Guy Burgess were interviewed for the first time by Mr. Richard Hughes of the *Sunday Times*.

*   *   *

Quimper folded the printouts and put them away in his pocket. He stood up and picked up the gun. "Thanks," he said to Kumar.

He kissed Vivian lightly on the lips. "You've been a great help," he said. "I don't know what I would have done without you."

"Quimper, where are you going?"

"Not far," Quimper said. "I have to make my report. I'll take a taxi."

41

"Stand calm, stand calm," Sergeant Lawrence cried, standing in the centre of the multi-coloured spotlight.

Of course no one did stand, or remain, calm. All of them had visions of sordid newspaper headlines and most of them had vivid impressions of the wrath of angry wives. The last thing they wanted to do when a uniformed policeman appeared on the stage of a strip club and asked them to remain calm, was to do precisely that.

In a ragged, untidy mass, the patrons of Le Chic Chick ran for the exit. At the top of the stairs was a solid phalanx of five policemen. The patrons of Le Chic Chick fell back in disordered array.

"Stand calm, stand calm," Sergeant Lawrence shouted. "All we want are your names and addresses."

This only provoked fresh panic. Men leapt over the bar, ran wildly round looking for doors or non-existent windows. Girls shrieked, tables overturned, glass shattered. Someone fell over the amplifier and boosted it to full volume. The spotlights focused on Sergeant Lawrence began to revolve faster and faster. The five policemen who had been at the top of the stairs entered the club.

In the midst of all this confusion, Harry Littledyke

remained calm. He knew there was one exit. The problem was how to get there. He gestured to Markovic to follow him and went across to the crazily revolving spotlight. In one swift movement he turned it off.

Sergeant Lawrence was plunged into instant darkness. With surprising agility, Littledyke leapt on to the stage dragging Markovic with him. He was damned if he was going to let the police trap either of them. Tonight he had delivered the final bit of information and tonight he had collected his final payment. Together they pounded into the greater darkness behind the stage and shut the door. Then they raced up the stairs.

Sergeant Lawrence heard the door slam and knew where they had gone. The stairs behind the stage led to Nicholas Maasten's office and Sergeant Lawrence knew there was no way out of there.

He waited until one of the constables had found a light switch and the room was once more bathed in a liverish glow. He waited till the noise had died down and his men were busy checking identifications and club membership cards and noting down names and addresses.

Then Sergeant Lawrence opened the door behind the stage and began climbing the stairs. It was an infernal nuisance, really. Sergeant Lawrence hated stairs.

"Nicholas," Littledyke cried, "you've got to help us. The cops are raiding the place."

"Yes," Ladislav Markovic said, "you've got to help us. If I get found out, they will kill me."

"Don't worry," Maasten said. "I'll help you." And wondered what the hell Carruthers expected him to do. Carruthers wouldn't want any scandal, Maasten was sure of that. But he was still wondering what the hell he was expected to do when Sergeant Lawrence lumbered in.

"What are you doing here?" Maasten asked. "This isn't even your manor!"

Sergeant Lawrence smiled, went over to the filing cabinet and helped himself to a glass of Scotch. "I'm West End Central," he said grinning.

Maasten said, "Glad you made it. You must feel quite at home there."

"Now, now, lad," Sergeant Lawrence said, "none of your lip."

"What are your people doing down here anyway, annoying my customers."

"If you didn't know, laddie, you've just been raided. We've got a warrant, laddie." He looked enquiringly at Maasten and sipped his Scotch. "You want to see the warrant?"

"I'll believe you," Maasten said.

Sergeant Lawrence smacked his lips. "Good Scotch, this. Wonder how a young fellow like you can afford it." He put the glass down and moved towards Littledyke and Markovic. "You," he snapped. "Both of you. What the hell do you mean by running up here when I ask you to stand calm?"

"Leave off," Maasten said. "They're friends of mine. We've been discussing business for the last half hour. Legal business."

"Really," Sergeant Lawrence said. "I could have sworn I saw these two chummies run across the stage and up your stairs. I suppose I must have imagined it."

"You did," Maasten said. "Anyway what's the raid for? We've got a licence and it hasn't gone twelve yet."

Sergeant Lawrence said, "Obscenity." Sergeant Lawrence said, "Lewdness." He pointed a stubby forefinger at Nicholas Maasten. "Soliciting. Keeping a disorderly house."

"It's an orderly house," Maasten protested. "I've had no complaints."

"Girls stripping on tables," Sergeant Lawrence said. "I call

227

that disorderly. Causing uproar at two o'clock in the morning. I call that disorderly. You'd better watch it, laddie. If I feel nasty about you, I'll throw in a living off immoral earnings charge too."

"I suppose," Maasten sighed, "I'd better call my lawyer."

"Don't touch that phone," Sergeant Lawrence shouted. He turned to Markovic. "You," he shouted. "What's your — "

Sergeant Lawrence's voice tailed off incredulously. For the second time in two weeks he'd found himself looking into the barrel of a gun.

"What's your name?" he asked gently.

Markovic said, "That is secret." With his free hand he gestured to the boarded up door. "Open," he said.

"But — "

"Open," Markovic screeched. His blink rate had gone up to seventy a minute.

Maasten got up and went to the door. It took a great deal of effort and a lot of battering, but finally he got it open.

"Goodbye, Harry," Markovic said.

"Just a sec, Ladislav, I'm coming with you."

"No you aren't," Sergeant Lawrence said, going very red in the face.

Markovic motioned Harry to get behind him, and still covering the room with his gun, they backed into a tiny cupboard-like room as dark as a coal cellar.

There was a thump. Indignantly Markovic strode out again. "That goes nowhere," he said accusingly to Maasten. Harry Littledyke followed, grimy and sheepish.

Maasten shrugged. "If I'd told you," he said, "you wouldn't have believed me."

He took a bunch of keys from his desk drawer and went over to the row of shelves behind his desk. "I only wish you'd ask me nicely," he said. He fumbled with the key

228

for a moment and then slid the shelf sideways revealing a great round hole in the wall, large enough for a man to get through.

"OK, Ladislav," he said, "off with you."

Harry moved smiling. "Not you," Maasten said, "you've got to stand up and be counted."

"Nicholas!"

"No, Harry. Not unless you want to get to Russia."

"But Nicholas — "

"Will you just leave it to me, Harry."

Sergeant Lawrence shouted, "You'll be charged with aiding and abetting."

"Oh, shut up, Lawrence," Maasten said. "Can't you see he's got a gun."

All they could see of Markovic now was the upper part of his body and his head with the lugubrious drooping moustache.

"Goodbye, Harry," he said and then in an accent that was a dead ringer for Littledyke's own. "It was great doing business with you."

Maasten moved the shelf back and sat down behind his desk. Sergeant Lawrence turned and darted for the door. Maasten touched a button underneath his desk and the door locked itself. "I'm just a bundle of surprises," Maasten said as Sergeant Lawrence whirled.

"Leave that phone alone," Sergeant Lawrence shouted. "And open the bloody door."

Maasten cradled the phone in his hand. "Lawrence," he said, "I'm trying to save you from a fate worse than death. How would you like to be an ordinary constable once again, pounding the beat, and you with ingrowing toenails. Believe me, Lawrence, when I place this call, you're going to go down on your fat little knees and thank me."

"Whom are you calling?" Lawrence asked suspiciously. "Why don't you have another drink and listen?"

The first person Maasten spoke to was David Carruthers. Then David Carruthers spoke to the Special Branch. And the Special Branch spoke to Sergeant Lawrence and asked him if he would mind leaving Nicholas Maasten alone. Except those weren't the words they used. The Special Branch can get exceptionally nasty when they feel anyone is poaching on what they consider to be their territory.

Sergeant Lawrence apologised and said he did not know. There should be a central register of these things. So that any clot could look at them, the Special Branch replied with heat. The Special Branch said they were coming round now and they would esteem it a great favour if Sergeant Lawrence and his men could be out of there before they got to the club. Except their choice of words was more vivid than that.

42

Angus McGregor looked from Vivian Ingleby to V. V. Kumar. "I'd never have believed it," he said. He thumped a clenched fist on the pile of printouts and repeated, "I'd never have believed it."

His red hair was more unkempt than ever and there was a shiny prickle of beard on his heavy jaw. He had dressed hurriedly, as soon as Kumar had phoned him about the tapes and now he was thinking he would have to see the Minister. "Where's Quimper?" he asked.

Vivian said, "I believe he was reporting to C."

McGregor said, "Ah! That's good." It meant there was one thing less for him to do and heaven knew there was enough. "Can you do something about getting him to a hospital?"

"I don't think it will be necessary," Vivian said. "He'll probably go back to his brother's. His brother is a surgeon."

"Yes," McGregor said, "I remember. I'll go round and see him tomorrow I think." He smiled tiredly at them. "Now I'd better talk to the Minister about expulsion orders." He came round the desk and stood in front of Vivian. "Thank you," he said, "and if you see Quimper before I do, tell him we are most grateful."

* * *

After Vivian and Kumar had left, McGregor sent for Carruthers and telephoned the Minister.

"Ninety-two expulsion orders. That's a lot to ask."

"I'm afraid it's necessary," McGregor said. "And we must serve them first thing in the morning."

"I suppose you have proof."

"Beyond all reasonable doubt," McGregor said.

He heard the Minister stifle a yawn. "Can you be in my office in half an hour?"

"Of course," McGregor said and put the phone down. Carruthers looked up from his printouts.

"Well," McGregor asked, "what do you think?"

"It's bad," Carruthers said.

"Worse than that," McGregor said bitterly. "Right under our very noses. They've made us look like pissed-on newts."

"It's not the Department's fault," Carruthers said. "MI5 should have been on to this months ago."

"We're all involved," McGregor growled. "It's a collective responsibility."

He sat down behind the desk and told Carruthers quickly about Quimper and Vivian and Jane Brewster and Hetherset. "I want you to take over Security," he said. "Quimper won't be fit for some time. I want all Records personnel re-vetted If they got at Hetherset, they might have got at others. Get whatever help you need."

"All right," Carruthers said.

"Talk to Quimper," McGregor said. "Find out exactly what happened in Wales. And who got Milner involved. You'll have to do something about the bodies."

"Right," Carruthers said.

"And David," McGregor said, "you'd better start now."

*   *   *

232

Going down in the lift to the basement, Kumar realised that the first thing they would do was check Records thoroughly. He had no doubt that if they found any irregularities they would hold him responsible. After all, he was now in charge. If he was going to be made head of Records, he'd have to make absolutely sure that there was nothing they could confront him with. Not even the printouts that Quimper had asked for.

When he got down into Records, Kumar made copies of the printouts Quimper had requested. Then he went back upstairs. The best thing to do, Kumar thought, was to tell McGregor all about it.

*   *   *

McGregor was about to leave when Kumar came in carrying the printouts. "I did these for Mr. Quimper," Kumar said. "I'm not sure that he had the authority."

McGregor took the printouts and spread them on the desk. After a while he said, "Damned impudence. Running a check on me." He twisted round so that Carruthers could read the printouts over his shoulder. "He's even checked you, David."

"The man's mad," Carruthers said.

McGregor kept on reading, and as he read he went very still. His broad flat face slowly filled with colour and the big freckled hands clenched and unclenched on the desk. When he had finished, he turned to Kumar. "Thank you," he said. "You did right to bring this to me."

Kumar hesitated. "I wanted to be sure it was in order, sir. Did Mr. Quimper — "

"Perfectly in order," McGregor said tightly.

As soon as Kumar left, Carruthers said, "Damn Quimper."

*   *   *

The two men stared at each other across the mass of paper. McGregor was the first to speak. "It's a hell of a situation," he said. He looked at his watch. "And I'm late for the Minister."

Carruthers said, "It's an R Section matter."

McGregor asked, "What about proof?"

Carruthers tapped the printouts. "That's enough."

McGregor said, "I can't authorise it, you know."

Carruthers said flatly, "I know. I'll get authorisation."

McGregor looked at his watch again. "I suppose," he said, "it's the only way."

Carruthers said, "Yes."

They went out of the office into the street. McGregor walked stiffly up to his car, got in and drove towards Whitehall. Carruthers went on to the car pool and took a black Humber. The sky above the square was lightening as he began to drive to Chequers.

43

MAASTEN POURED LITTLEDYKE A STIFF DRINK. "OK, Harry," he said, "give it to me straight."

"Haven't I always, Nicholas?"

"No." He looked at his watch. "The police will be here any moment now. They're not your local friendly copper like Sergeant Lawrence. These boys are from the Special Branch. They're heavies."

Harry licked his lips and held out his glass. "I haven't done anything," he said.

Nicholas poured. "Tell me about Markovic."

"I don't know what to say, Nicholas."

"Try it from the beginning," Maasten said.

Harry gulped his drink. "Well, there was this pukka geezer, striped suit and all. Said he was from the Air Ministry and could I help the government. Said he knew you, Nicholas, that you'd recommended me, you know. He said we were having a bit of difficulty selling the Concorde like, and would I like to help."

"Harry," Maasten asked softly. "Just when did you become a patriot?"

"Now, you don't go thinking nasty things about me, Nicholas. I've always been a patriot. Fought in the bleeding war too, didn't I!"

235

"There wasn't much of a war in Skye," Maasten pointed out.

Harry looked deflated. "Couldn't help where they sent me, could I," he muttered.

"No," Maasten said. "I suppose not. Anyway what about this geezer?"

"Proper toff he was and all. I'll just hev a coffee, thank yew. I don't heppen to like treacle tart."

"What did he want you to do?"

"He wanted me to leak some information to the Russkis. Like how well the Concorde was doing, that kind of thing. It would make them interested, he said, and if the Russkis bought it, he said, then Pan American would have no alternative."

"How much did he offer you?" Maasten asked.

"Two hundred knicker and what I could squeeze out of the Russkis."

"What did they pay?"

Harry hesitated. In a small voice he said, "Two and a half grand."

"For information they could pick up from the *Daily Telegraph* reference library."

"This was Top Secret stuff," Harry protested. "Classified grade one."

Maasten held out his hand. "Let me see."

Reluctantly Harry gave him a sheaf of papers. Maasten looked at them. A brief look was enough.

"Harry," Maasten said, "do you know what you have done?"

"What have I done?"

"You've just given the Russkis all the information on the Sepecat Cougar, a mach-two single-seat fighter built by Aerospatiel and BAC."

236

"Bleeding hell, Nicholas, the man said it was the Concorde."

"There is," Maasten said, "a substantial difference." Once more he got up and slid the shelves back. "Harry," he asked, "they paid you the two and a half thousand smackers did they?"

Harry hesitated and said, "Yuss. Got the last instalment today."

"You haven't spent it or anything, have you?"

"Spent about five hundred pounds of it," Harry admitted shamefully. "A few drinks with the boys, and a little bit on the dogs . . ."

"Harry," Maasten asked, "have you a good travel agent?"

"Haven't got one, Nicholas. Always go to Blackpool for me — "

"Get one," Maasten advised. "Fast. And book yourself on a long, long holiday, very far from either England or France."

"Nicholas, where could I go?"

"Try Australia," Maasten suggested. "There's a lot of space there, where a man can lose himself."

After Harry had left. Maasten called David Carruthers. The girl at the other end recognised his voice and was terribly sorry but David Carruthers simply would not be available for six hours or so. He was on an extremely important assignment. It had to do with something called the Kiriov tapes.

Maasten put the phone down and lit one more cigarette. There was no point in his talking to the Special Branch alone. They might not believe him, and worse, they might even get the wrong idea. The only thing he could do was to wait for David Carruthers.

Maasten extinguished his cigarette and emptied the ashtray. Then he turned off the lights and followed Markovic and Littledyke through the hole in the wall.

44

QUIMPER RODE IN THE TAXI right up to the white-painted door and got out. He gave the driver fifty pence and did not bother to enter it in his notebook. He went up the steps and knocked.

As usual he was admitted without question. As usual C was waiting for him in the vast reception room with the oil paintings by Sir Winston Churchill on the walls.

"Quimper," he said. Then concerned, "You're hurt."

"It isn't serious," Quimper said.

C asked, "Would you like a drink?"

Quimper's shoulder was more painful now as the effect of the drug Hugh had given him started to wear off. "Some Scotch, sir. If you don't mind."

"Scotch eh! Of course. Of course."

C walked over to the drinks trolley and poured. "Ice? Water? Soda?"

"Just ice," Quimper said and added, "please."

C handed him his drink and they both sat down facing each other. Quimper took the printouts from his jacket and placed them on the table. "I've got the Kiriov tapes back, sir."

"Did you, Quimper? Oh, splendid. That's absolutely splendid."

"I've left them with Records to be copied and circulated."

"Was that wise, Quimper? I mean, we have to think of Security."

Quimper said, "The last time, sir, we thought too much about Security."

C thought that over, the round, shaggy head buried in the plump shoulders. Finally he said, "Humph! I suppose you're right. But it's restricted access only?"

"Yes," Quimper said.

"Good. Very good." C looked up at Quimper. "Congratulations," he said. "Who had them?"

"One of the technicians, sir. Alistair Hetherset. He was a member of a suspect political organisation and he thought that Kiriov had implicated this organisation."

"So he took the tapes, eh Quimper?"

"Yes. On the night in question, Pute left early. Pute's assistant was delayed because the battery in his car had been stolen. Hetherset had ample opportunity."

"Looks more than that, Quimper, eh what. You'll have to tighten up Security in Records. Can't have chappies walking in and out with highly secret documents in their briefcases, what."

"No," Quimper said. "One can't."

"This chap Hetherset hadn't damaged the tapes in any way?"

"Apparently not," Quimper said.

"Do you know exactly what was on the tapes, Quimper?"

"Yes," Quimper said. "Amongst other things, Kiriov named about twenty diplomats who were part of a spy ring. I suppose tomorrow you'll have to ask for their expulsion."

239

"Do you really think that, Quimper? Oh dear! It'll be a busy day tomorrow." C looked pointedly at his watch.

Quimper said, "I don't think Pute was directly involved, sir. I don't believe Pute committed suicide."

"Don't you, Quimper?"

"Pute was a scrupulous person. He would never have prepared duplicate tapes unless he'd been ordered to do so. I think the same person who gave Pute those orders, told Harvey Milner where he could find Pute."

"I've seen the report on Pute's death. It is pretty conclusive, you know. Pute was a spy. Pretty conclusive, eh what?" C gripped the arms of his chair preparatory to standing up.

Quimper said, "There's something else, sir. Harvey Milner."

"Harvey Milner, oh yes."

"He was a professional gunman, sir. A freelance. Why did you hire him, sir?"

"Oh, Carruthers must have said we were short handed or something. Could always use an extra gun."

"R Section doesn't need to hire gunmen," Quimper said. "They've got enough gunmen on their staff. You engaged Milner, didn't you, sir?"

"Yes," C said. "I'm sure you realise that sometimes there is a reason that one is unable to divulge. Need to know, Quimper, need to know. That's the principle every intelligence operation works on."

"Oh, yes it works all right," Quimper answered. "For hiring a ghost from the McCarthy era. For hiring someone like Milner and no questions asked. Did you know, sir, that Milner was a psychopath. That he liked killing? That he needed to kill? Did you know that he killed Henry Pute and Alistair Hetherset and Hetherset's girlfriend, Jane Brewster? That he liked killing so much even the CIA wouldn't use him."

"Oh, Quimper, really!"

"I had to kill Milner, sir, even though he was one of ours. Even though he was acting under orders."

C frowned. "That's damn serious," he said. "Whose orders?"

Quimper took out the Smith and Wesson. "Yours," he said, "sir."

*   *   *

C stared at Quimper, eyebrows knitted together in a steely-grey web. "Quimper," he asked incredulously, "have you gone mad?"

"It was you who told Hetherset about the Gnomes, wasn't it?"

"I don't know what you are talking about."

"The Red Gnomes, sir. A political organisation. An offshoot of the Dutch Kabouters. Hetherset was a member and you had him warned that they were implicated by the Kiriov tapes."

"Honestly, Quimper, I think you should get to bed. You've done a splendid job. We'll talk this over in the morning."

"No," Quimper said. "It was you who killed Amory wasn't it? You couldn't use Milner, because Milner had worked with Amory and even he would have suspected something. Milner was rabid enough to be convinced that Pute and Hetherset were spies. But it wouldn't have worked with Amory, would it? So you had to do it yourself."

C said, "I haven't shot anything in years, except grouse."

Quimper sipped his whisky. "At first I thought it was Carruthers," he said. "Carruthers is an easy man to hate. But the dum-dums meant that it had to be someone who wasn't professional. Someone who knew how good Amory was and wanted to be absolutely certain of stopping him with one shot."

241

C said, "Have you thought that the Russians might be running short of professionals?"

Quimper said, "Not so," and hefted the gun in his fist. "You were a good friend of Kim Philby's, weren't you, sir?" he asked.

C coloured. "I knew the man, yes. I believe he once worked under me. In Washington." C leaned forward. "Are you sure you're all right, Quimper? Shall I get a doctor to look at your wound? Don't you think you should be in hospital?"

Quimper asked, "Did you know Philby terribly well? And what about the other two?"

C said, "What the devil has Philby got to do with this? He went over years ago."

"Yes," Quimper said, "and he was a damn sight more than a casual acquaintance in Washington. You were both in Cambridge at the same time. You were both members of the Anglo-German Fellowship."

"That was a long time ago," C said tightly.

"Yes," Quimper said, "it was."

Quimper took a sip of Scotch. "I knew Philby too," he said. "In Cyprus. We were good friends in Cyprus. Once he might even have saved my life. You remember? After I was brought back to London I made a report on it."

"I don't remember every single detail that is on your personal file."

"You remembered enough to tell Milner about Beirut, didn't you?"

C said, "But I didn't."

"Milner knew about Beirut," Quimper said. "He thought I was a spy too. Or a coward." Quimper laughed. "There are only three people who know about Beirut. McGregor, Carruthers and yourself."

C said, "Quimper, I can see what you're leading up to and I find it indescribably boring. We are both tired and it is quite late. Why don't you put that gun away and let's both get some sleep, eh!"

Quimper said, "The last time I saw Philby was in Beirut, on January 19th, 1963. Do you remember January 1963?" he asked. "You gave me orders to kill Philby."

C sighed. "Quimper, this is absolutely ridiculous."

"Not ridiculous. Clever. Sending me to Beirut was very clever. Picking me was even cleverer. You *knew* we had worked together. You knew I *liked* him. That's why the job was kept so secret. I had no time to prepare. I didn't even know whom I was supposed to kill until I saw him."

Quimper moved his left arm awkwardly and sipped the Scotch. "You made damn sure I couldn't refuse that assignment," he said. "You couldn't risk the Department sending someone else. Damn it, you bastard, you wanted me to fail."

"Put that gun away, Quimper," C said.

"In January 1963 Philby was working in Beirut, for the *Observer* and the *Economist*. He didn't know that Dolnytsin — if that was his real name — had defected from the KGB in Helsinki. Philby didn't know that Dolnytsin had been interrogated by the SIS and the CIA and that he had put the finger on Philby."

Quimper's arm was beginning to hurt. He took another sip of Scotch, hoping it would drown the pain. "There was nothing you could do about Dolnytsin was there? There was no way you could get at him. The first you knew about it was when an SIS agent was sent to Beirut to question Philby. You couldn't understand why Philby stayed in Beirut after that. Especially after a second agent was sent to interrogate him."

Quimper laughed. "You thought that Philby had got too

complacent. You remembered that ten years previously he had been cross-examined by Helenus Milmo and had survived. You thought that Philby must feel that this was just another episode. That it would end like all the others had ended and that it would be foolish for him to run away. Philby was much too closely watched for you to risk sending him a message. You couldn't say to him that his period of usefulness had ended, that you couldn't protect him any more. So you used me." Quimper laughed again. "The assassin with a blank bullet."

C said, "Rubbish. Absolute rubbish."

Quimper sipped more Scotch.

C said, "I wonder if you realise the seriousness of what you've just said. I wonder, Quimper, if you realise the seriousness of what you are now doing. You realise I could break you for this, break you in so many tiny pieces that you'll never be a whole man again."

"Don't bother," Quimper said. "That's already been done." He gave a short laugh. "Applied psychology, isn't that what you call it? And nothing's changed has it? Me in 1963, now Pute and Hetherset and even poor bloody Milner." He rested his gunhand on the arm of the chair. "I'm going to kill you," he said.

C remained impassive. "You haven't any proof," he said.

"And you, have you always had proof when you gave orders for someone to be removed?"

"It's different," C said, "from this side of the desk. I was doing what I thought necessary for my country."

"Which country?" Quimper asked.

C leaned back in his chair. For the first time he picked up his Scotch and drank it, sipping delicately. They might have been at his club, discussing anthropology. "You know, Quimper, I've been in Intelligence for nearly thirty-five years.

In that time I've acquired a vast amount of experience, a vast amount of knowledge. It isn't the kind of thing that goes down on one's file. It's more ephemeral, if you like, than that. And much much more valuable. You know, Adrian, it's strange. When I retire it will be at least ten years before that knowledge is valueless, it will take them at least ten years to de-brief me." He looked directly at Quimper and smiled. "You are about to dispose of all that in one split second." He gripped the arm of the chair and leaned forward. "Tell me, Adrian, what if you are wrong? Can you stand the responsibility?"

"Keep seated," Quimper said, "don't move towards me."

"I must say you've prepared a jolly decent case," C said. "Very thorough even though it's entirely circumstantial. Have you reflected, Adrian. That in Intelligence, there is no such thing as the truth. It appears and disappears like a shadow, and what is true is only true for one time. You have double agents, and triple agents, even quadruple agents. The sad thing is that you never, ever, know."

C paused and sipped his Scotch. "You used to be in the police, Adrian. Think carefully, now. If I were in the dock, could you get a conviction on the evidence you have just produced? Of course, you might say that we are not in a court of law. That justice doesn't apply. But you've got to believe that, Adrian, or believe in the justice and the rightness of things. You've sworn to uphold the law, not take it into your own hands." C stood up. "Besides," he said, "if you were to kill me, you could be very, very wrong. You'd never know and that is a most terrible responsibility."

"Get away from me," Quimper snapped. "Get away or I'll shoot."

"Shoot, Adrian, and risk killing an innocent man?" C was

245

walking towards Quimper now. "Shoot, Adrian, and risk the uncertainty, the not knowing?"

C towered over him. Quimper looked into the calm relentless face, the voice flowing gently over him in rolling cadences.

"Adrian," C said, "don't abuse the innocent."

Quimper's finger tightened around the trigger. C was right up against him, now. "Not the innocent, especially not the innocent." Quimper's finger hesitated.

Froze.

C hit him on his wounded shoulder. Sharp, breath-stopping incisions of pain knifed through him. Quimper gasped, felt the floor reel. C's hand closed on his gun. For a moment they struggled. Then C speared his wounded shoulder again. Quimper felt it start to bleed, hot and wet and clinging. C was dragging at him now and Quimper let go and fell on the polished floor.

C said, "I could kill you now, but it would be impossible to explain. Just as it would be impossible for you to explain your theories about me. No one would believe either of us."

Slowly, Quimper sat up.

"Goodbye, Quimper," C said. "Good luck."

*   *   *

Outside in the warm dark night, Quimper could not believe that it was over. That it had ended so quickly, so simply, so inconclusively. He went up the street, clutching his shoulder, feeling the blood collecting in his palm. Damn it, he knew. There were some things one didn't need proof for. Some things for which intuition and emotion and circumstances were enough. Now, Quimper thought, C knew that he knew.

Quimper thought of America. He had to get away. It

246

would be good to see Marcia and his grandchildren. He could go to America, to remember Amaryk.

He wondered how soon it would be before he came across Milner and remembered that Milner was dead. It would be someone like Milner, he thought.

He waited a long time in the dark street for a taxi.

45

IT WAS TWO MINUTES PAST TWELVE when McGregor came into Carruthers's office. A fine growth of red and white fuzz covered his cheeks and his clothes were badly rumpled. "All done," he said. "They've kicked them all out. Every single one of them." He looked anxiously at Carruthers. "How about you?"

Carruthers said, "I have authorisation."

McGregor asked, "Whom will you send?"

"I'll go myself. I'm due there in twenty minutes."

* * *

Markovic stared unbelievingly at the piece of paper in his hand. He was being expelled from Britain and he couldn't believe it. He had got away from the club without being found out so there was no reason for the British to kick him out. He would protest, he thought, before he realised that it was impossible.

It was only later that afternoon that he was told that ninety of his colleagues were also being expelled. They were mostly KGB men and he didn't like to be associated with them at all.

"Just in time," the air attaché said. "Your information

248

came just in time. It is very valuable and you will be suitably rewarded."

Markovic hoped that they would give him a flat of his own in Moscow. With central heating.

"Goodbye," the air attaché said. "You are leaving on the five o'clock flight. It is an Ilyushin IL-62. It will be a good flight."

46

As Carruthers walked into the large reception room, lined with pictures of former prime ministers, C came out of the small anteroom he used as an office.

"David," he said and pointed to the suite of leather armchairs. "Sit down. I suppose you've come about the Kiriov tapes."

Carruthers stayed where he was. "Yes," he said.

C stopped and for a moment the two men stared at each other.

Carruthers said, "We have a meeting with the Minister. I have a car outside."

C hesitated. "I didn't know that," he said and began to walk slowly towards his office. "I'd better check my diary."

Carruthers dropped his hand into his pocket and took out the gun. "Let's go," he said. "Quietly."

C turned and stared. His eyes ranged quietly over Carruthers, taking in the pale brown suit and the hard translucent eyes. Finally they rested on the gun in Carruthers's hand. It was a Browning 9 mm Hi-power automatic. C said softly, "So it was you."

Carruthers nodded.

C shook his head slowly in disbelief. "I should have

known," he said, still speaking softly. "I should have known. It was you who insisted we hire Milner. It was you who had the ingenious idea of sending Quimper to Beirut to assassinate Philby. Why did you hire Milner?"

"He was grateful for the work," Carruthers said.

"And loyal, I suppose."

"He was loyal to me."

"Like one of Pavlov's dogs," C said.

Carruthers said, "We'd better go now."

"Quimper?" C asked. "Is he one of yours?"

"No," Carruthers said. "He was working on his own. But he created the situation I needed." He looked down at the gun. "To do this."

C asked, "Dum-dums?"

Carruthers nodded.

"You needed them for Amory?"

"Amory was good. He wouldn't have given me a second chance. Besides I didn't want it to look professional."

"How long," C asked, "have you been with them?"

"Always," Carruthers said. He gestured with the gun. "Let's go."

C went up to a rack on the wall and put on a light grey raincoat. "I suppose it's wet outside," he said and looked fondly around the room. Then he turned back to Carruthers. "I suppose there is no point in my saying anything."

"None at all," Carruthers said.

C began to walk out of the room. Suddenly, remembering something, he stopped and turned. "One moment," he said. "I left the dispatch box open." He took out a large key and smiled hesitantly at Carruthers. "Habit," he said. "I must lock it."

Carruthers stepped aside and allowed C to precede him into the anteroom. The office was small and crowded and on C's

251

desk was a large red box with a heavy coat of arms on its lid. C picked up the box and turned round, holding it in front of his chest, facing Carruthers.

"I've always liked this box," C said. "It was a kind of symbol." He inserted the key into the lock. "Never used it much you know, except for keeping sandwiches." He looked across the box at Carruthers. "I'd better get rid of them, I suppose. It wouldn't look good, afterwards."

He opened the lid and thrust his hand into the box. Carruthers heard the rustle of paper. The next second the box exploded.

C reeled back pulling his arm away, fingers still twisted round the butt of the S and W .38 Special. Carruthers stared incredulously at the blood blossoming on his pale brown jacket. C fired again, as he fell against the desk. Carruthers's head jerked back. A hole appeared in his throat, filling rapidly with blood. Glassy-eyed, his knees crumpled and he sagged on to the floor, gasping. C stepped right up to him and shot him once more in the head.

47

MAASTEN LEVELLED THE AERO COMMANDER at fifteen thousand feet and thought it was still as sluggish as he remembered it, from the old Air Chartel days. He clicked a lighter into flame, lit a cigarette and turned to face his passenger, strapped in the co-pilot's seat. "You've got guts," he said, "trying to nail C."

Adrian Quimper said, "I never thought it could be Carruthers. The printout didn't fit him."

"Computers are tools," Maasten said, "they do what you want them to do. At least that's what my accountant says."

Quimper said, "Funny how no-one knew about Carruthers."

Maasten said, "We do now. His real name was Mikajil Golenowski. Trust a foreigner to change his name to Carruthers."

Maasten checked his reading and altered course slightly. "We're going to Spain," he said, "McGregor wants you out of the way for a bit and you'll have a chance to rest up." He smiled at Quimper. "You'll like it in Spain," he promised. "You'll be staying at the castle de Maerez. It will be very restful."

Quimper asked, "I wonder why Carruthers didn't destroy the tapes?"

Vivian came into the cockpit from behind them, carrying steaming mugs of tea. "Stop thinking about it, Adrian," she said. "It's all over."

"They wanted time to get out the information on the Sepecat Cougar," Maasten said.

Quimper frowned. "But it doesn't make sense. They've lost nearly one hundred operatives."

Maasten looked out of the glass canopy into the searing blue sky. "They were expendable," he said. "Sooner or later we would have found out about them anyway. And sooner or later they will be replaced." He gave Quimper a wry grin. "Now they've got an excuse to expel some of our people from Moscow."

Quimper asked, "And what about Pute and Hetherset? Were they expendable too?"

"Spying," Nichcolas Maasten said, "is a very dirty business."